STORM'S CUT

AMELIA STORM SERIES: BOOK TEN

MARY STONE

AMY WILSON

DESCRIPTION

The first cut is the deepest.

Murderers never take a break, so when the body of a twenty-nine-year-old middle school gym teacher is discovered, Special Agents Amelia Storm and Zane Palmer are called in to help the Violent Crimes Division with one of their most puzzling cases to date. Because this isn't just a random crime...

It's far more bizarre.

The latest victim is the fifth to be found dumped in a rural area south of Chicago. The victims have little in common, except one thing...their internal organs have been removed with a precision that only a surgeon could achieve.

Is this the work of a deranged serial killer, an organ trafficker, or God forbid, both? Or could one of Chicago's criminal organizations be involved?

Despite their investigation yielding one dead end after another, Amelia is determined to keep digging. Because she has no doubt that the murderer will strike again, and soon...unless she stops them first.

From the wickedly dark minds of Mary Stone and Amy Wilson comes Storm's Cut, book ten of the Amelia Storm Series that will make you realize that those sworn to protect can inflict the most harm.

1

The faint chill of the evening breeze left a series of goose bumps along the exposed skin of Kari Hobill's forearms. It was early April, and the weather had begun to warm, but the air still carried a cool bite, as if trying to hold on to winter a little bit longer. She paused at the start of the walking trail that snaked through the partially wooded park, pulling in a deep breath to savor the bright scents of spring.

Out here in the suburbs bordering Chicago, Kari could fully enjoy the start of her favorite season. Sure, the city had its perks, and not all the smells were bad—she distinctly recalled how much she'd loved to walk past a locally owned bakery on her lunch breaks and catch a whiff of the delectable treats—but for the most part, Kari didn't miss the hustle and bustle.

Though there were plenty of parks where she could go for a walk or a run, the city always carried the risk of being jumped, mugged, or worse. Kari had made a habit of carrying pepper spray, and even considered a Taser at one point, but they weren't legal in the state of Illinois. Chances were, she didn't need to go to such lengths out here in the 'burbs, but old habits died hard. Nearly a decade in Chicago had ingrained caution in her.

However, the main aspect of Chicago she didn't miss was the memory of the time she'd spent with her ex-husband, Clint Haney. Six months ago, before the divorce was even finalized, Kari had packed up and moved to a sleepy suburb where her father and a couple of family friends lived.

She'd never envisioned herself as the type of person to settle down in a place filled with cookie-cutter houses and manicured lawns, but to her surprise, she enjoyed the quiet lifestyle. She didn't quite have the money to buy a house, but her rental in suburbia was comfortable.

As a thirty-year-old social worker, her days of living among her clients in the city had come and gone. After a long and sometimes rewarding day of helping folks, the last thing Kari wanted was to meet one of her clients while waiting for the L, the elevated train system in Chicago. Sure, she was still young, still had a full life ahead of her, but that life no longer involved an endless cluster of strangers.

Shaking off her musings, Kari took another deep breath as she hopped from one foot to the other. Her head was all sorts of jumbled right now, and she knew a good run at dusk was just what she needed to get her thoughts to cooperate.

Smile, Kari. Fake it 'til you make it, remember?

She stretched both arms above her head and grinned. While bending forward, she flexed one foot, then the other to get her hammies stretched. A pre-run ritual to loosen up her muscles.

Checking the parking lot to make sure it was all clear—a habit from days gone by—she took comfort that her cherry-red Hyundai was the only vehicle present. Pressing her lips together, she made her way to the smooth sidewalk that would take her through a copse of trees, over a small creek, and through a grassy field before looping around back to the parking lot.

"All right. Let's do this."

She took off at a modest jog. Fitness hadn't always been a priority for Kari. In fact, she'd detested exercise until three years ago, when she'd gone to the gym with a friend from college in an effort to feel less self-conscious. Ironically, of the two of them, Kari had been the one who wound up delving into a full-on lifestyle change. She'd dropped three dress sizes since then and gained a world of confidence.

Even as her feet pounded the ground and her breathing accelerated, Kari let out a quiet snort, thinking about her old friend. She hadn't seen her in forever. She made a note to call her later in the week, or at least text to catch up.

Running was the activity she used to process the random, anxious energy coursing through her brain. She envisioned herself leaving the thoughts behind as she ran, using the mindset to motivate herself. Whoever said running from your problems never solved anything was wrong, at least in Kari's case.

Crisscrossed branches of leafless trees shaded the path and cut through the warmth of the waning sunlight. Despite the sheen of sweat beginning to form on her skin, a chill skittered down Kari's back. The scene was peaceful enough, but shifting from sunlight to shade always gave her a jolt of paranoia.

It's okay. I've got mace, and I've got this.

Shaking off the baseless anxiety, Kari almost leapt out of her skin at the crackles of dried grass and leaves to her right. Her head whipped to the side where trees and weeds bordered the creek that meandered through the park. Just ahead of her, the shadowy figure of a man emerged from behind the trunk of a tall oak, and Kari's hand shot straight to the mace in her pocket as she skidded to a stop. Every muscle tensed in preparation for potential danger.

This is a park. Other people come here too. But what is he doing down by the creek? There's at least a ten-foot drop to the water. Was he hiding there?

She clenched her jaw. Whoever the young man was, he still seemed oblivious to her presence. His gaze was fixed on an object in his hand—his phone, she assumed.

Was he homeless? No, Kari could tell his clothes were clean, maybe even new. His dark blond hair was shaggy but not dirty.

A Peeping Tom?

She grimaced.

Back when she and Clint were still together, she and a couple of other women in their apartment complex had been the object of a creeper's obsession. Eventually, he was caught by the police, but the violation of privacy had left an emotional scar. Whenever she spotted a man behaving strangely, she jumped to the worst-case scenario.

The person in front of her wasn't a man, though. He was more like a kid. Was he even eighteen? His face was clean-shaven, so maybe he just *appeared* young.

Kari cleared her throat to announce her presence.

Shoulders going rigid, the young man froze in place as his pale blue eyes snapped up to meet hers. All the emotions that had just rushed through Kari's mind—uncertainty, worry, and yes, even a little fear—flashed over his face in a split second.

Unless he was a very good actor, she'd apparently caught him just as off guard as he'd caught her.

His Adam's apple bobbed as he swallowed. "H-hello. Sorry, you, uh," he cleared his throat, straightening his back as he did, "surprised me a little bit. I didn't see any cars in the parking lot when I got here, so I assumed I was alone."

What on earth was a kid his age doing traipsing around near a creek bed at six thirty on a Saturday evening? Shouldn't he be out partying or playing video games with his friends? Or meeting a girl at the park so they could make out?

Of course, he could be older than he looked, she knew. At shorter than five feet and barely a hundred pounds, Kari had been mistaken for a child on more than one occasion.

Kari loosened her death grip on the mace. "You're out here alone?"

A flush crept up the kid's cheeks, and Kari was struck with a jolt of the same embarrassment for her accusatory tone. "Um, my mom dropped me off while she ran to the store."

"Sorry. I didn't mean to sound rude. It's just...weird."

He let out a nervous laugh. "It is kinda weird, isn't it?" He lifted his phone. "I'm taking some pictures for my science class. We're studying botany right now."

"Taking pictures of what? All the plants are still dead." Kari silently cursed herself for how much edginess was left in her voice. Clearly, small talk with strangers outside her job was something she needed to work on.

Rather than appearing offended, the kid's expression brightened. "That's what I said when he gave us the assignment. I'm glad someone else thinks this is dumb too. But I guess not all the plants are *dead*-dead. Some of them will be growing again in a few weeks, and I'm supposed to come back and take more pictures then."

His explanation made sense. Kari was about twelve years removed from high school, but she could still recall the bizarre projects some of her teachers had assigned.

"Anyway, um, it was nice to meet you." The kid glanced at his phone. "But I better go. I've got a few more pictures to take before Mom picks me up."

Kari forced an amiable smile onto her face. "Nice to meet you too. Good luck with your project."

With a wave of his hand, the young man headed back down into the trees.

Kari waited a beat before she let out a long sigh. Annoyed at her paranoia, she rolled her shoulders and returned to a slow jog.

To her relief, the remainder of her run was uneventful. No other students were skulking in the grass taking photos for one of their assignments. In fact, Kari didn't come across another soul. Her only companions were the birds and squirrels chattering in the leafless trees.

Still, despite the near certainty she was alone, Kari couldn't shake the creepy-crawly sensation that someone was watching her.

Was the kid taking pictures of dead plants secretly a budding serial killer? Kari had seen enough news articles to know even young kids were capable of despicable acts.

Should she have asked him more questions?

Her stomach twisted as she crested the gentle slope leading to the parking lot. Maybe he'd been out searching for his next victim, and he'd show up at her house later that night to...

Stop it. You're being ridiculous. He's just a kid working on a project for his class.

Perhaps, but Kari's racing mind wouldn't be put to rest until she was home behind a locked door with a baseball bat nearby.

Kari peered at the shrubs and trees bordering the parking lot, partially convinced an assailant was lurking, waiting for the perfect moment to strike. Her calves burned from the exertion of the run, but she was so absorbed in monitoring her surroundings she barely noticed the unpleasant sensation.

Not watching the path ahead, she bowled over a man standing where the walking trail met the sidewalk leading to the parking lot. Adrenaline surged through her body.

"Shit." Immediately, she regretted swearing, a leftover admonition from her childhood that cursing showed a lack of eloquence.

Though she half expected to find the "roadblock" to be the same kid from earlier, it wasn't. As this new strange man spun around to face her, eyes wide with surprise, she was struck with the notion they'd crossed paths before today. For the life of her, she couldn't recall where she'd seen him, though.

Resting a hand over his heart, the stranger sucked in a deep breath and offered her an uneasy smile. "Holy smokes, miss, you just about scared the daylights out of me."

The hairs on the back of Kari's neck rose to attention.

By her best guess, he was in his forties or fifties. Did older guys really talk like that, or was he a cartoon character? Kari's dad was pushing sixty, and he definitely didn't use the same turns of phrase as this man.

Kari licked her lips as she forced her way past the rampant sense of apprehension. "Sorry. I must've been spacing out. I didn't even see you."

With a grin, he waved a dismissive hand. "All's well that ends well. Say, what are you doing out here so close to nightfall? Are you alone?"

Alarm bells sounded off in Kari's head with every *thud* of her pulse.

Why did he want to know if she was alone? She found it hard to believe a strange man standing at the edge of a parking lot cared about her welfare. Besides, her car was *right there*. She was about to leave, and he was the only thing barring her path. As nonchalantly as possible, Kari reached into the pocket where she kept her mace.

Better safe than sorry.

"Out for a run. Was just about to head home." Even as the blood drummed in her ears, she kept her expression as neutral as possible. Not friendly, not edgy, just neutral.

He stuffed both hands in the pockets of his light jacket. Breathing deeply, he nodded his approval. "It's a great day to be outside. Probably one of the nicest days we've had yet this spring, don't you think?"

Kari fought to return his pleasant expression, but her face was wooden and stiff. All she wanted to do was leave. "Yeah, it sure is. Listen, um, I don't want to seem rude, but I was just about to head home. I'm all sweaty, and dinner is calling, you know?"

Though he acted like he understood, he didn't move. "Of course. Say, did you see someone else around while you were on that trail? Someone down that way by the creek. I'm supposed to be picking up a friend." He pointed in the direction from which she'd come. His face brightened and he waved. "Hey!"

She turned, and immediately realized her mistake.

In the corner of her eye, she caught a flicker of movement and her instincts screamed at her to *run*. She tried, but time slowed, and the air thickened to the consistency of cold molasses as she turned to assess the threat.

It was real this time. Not some figment of her overactive imagination.

Before she could scream or even raise her hands in defense, a fist slammed into her neck. A second later, a nest of bees seemed to attack her throat. By the time Kari spotted the syringe in his grasp, it was too late.

Her vision swam like the world had become a watercolor painting. Knees wobbling, she gasped for air as she struggled to maintain her balance.

Fight it. Whatever it is, fight, dammit!

Grating her teeth, she willed her hand to free the mace from her pocket. Her fingers started to cooperate, giving her faint hope. She'd heard plenty of stories about adrenaline coming to the rescue of people in dire straits.

Maybe, just maybe…

Her knees buckled as darkness nibbled at the corners of her vision. As she pitched forward to face-plant on the sidewalk, a strong arm circled around her waist and held her upright.

"There, there, Kari. Careful now. I've got great plans for you, my dear."

Plans? How does he know my name?

She opened her mouth to protest, but all that came out was a meager groan before darkness took over.

2

Blowing on the steaming mug of coffee in her hands, Special Agent Amelia Storm took a seat in a mesh-backed office chair beside Agent Zane Palmer. Despite savoring the delicious coffee from the machine gifted to them when Agent Journey Russo and her sister, Michelle Timmer, had decided to leave Chicago, Amelia's thoughts drifted back to darker memories.

It had been about nine months since Special Agent Joseph Larson had abducted Michelle. Her subsequent brutal assaults—by both Joseph and Brian "The Shark" Kolthoff—left physical and psychological wounds that would take time and therapy for Michelle to heal. This, Amelia knew all too well. Michelle and Journey had departed Chicago for a fresh start, and Amelia sincerely hoped they'd thrive in a new setting.

In a desperate move after Michelle's rescue, Joseph kidnapped Amelia's sister-in-law, Joanna, and took her to a lake house. The corrupt, misogynistic murderer had under-estimated Amelia, however, and she used his arrogance to her advantage. While they might never uncover all the secrets that died with Joseph at the lake house, Amelia was grateful to have saved Jo and closed that chapter.

Zane shifted in his seat next to Amelia and she refocused on the present. They'd been called in to help a couple of their fellow agents, Sherry Cowen and Dean Steelman, with a puzzling case. A body had just been recovered in rural Illinois and was currently on its way to the Cook County Medical Examiner's Office. The phone call from Amelia and Zane's immediate superior, Supervisory Special Agent Spencer Corsaw, hadn't yielded much detail about the case, only that the SSA from Violent Crimes had asked for their help.

Even on a Sunday evening, murderers didn't take a break.

At least Journey and Michelle gave us a new coffee maker for the breakroom. Bye, bye to liquid tar.

Smiling, Amelia took a sip of the rich, dark, silky brew.

"Michelle and Journey must have *really* hated the coffee here."

Zane's remark made Amelia wonder if he could read minds, but in reality, he just knew her well enough to figure out what she was thinking when she smiled into her coffee mug.

Amelia and Zane had worked together in the FBI's Organized Crime Division for nearly a year. During their time together in the Chicago Field Office, they'd forged a strong friendship that had eventually turned romantic.

The evolution of their dynamic was no real surprise to Amelia, but what *did* surprise her was how seamless the entire transition had been. And bringing Jasmine Keaton, the Special Agent in Charge of the Chicago Field Office, up to speed had been a breeze. There were a few caveats to dating a coworker in a job like Amelia's—they were discouraged from working potentially dangerous field assignments together, for instance—but for the most part, nothing about their lives in the office had changed.

As the door to the conference room creaked open behind Amelia, she swiveled in her chair to face the newcomers. Her spirit lightened at the sight of Agents Sherry Cowen and Dean Steelman. She and Zane had first worked with the Violent Crimes agents on a case in rural Illinois in the fall of the previous year, and since then, they'd collaborated on a handful of other investigations.

Though Sherry was an inch taller than Amelia's five-eight frame, she still stood a good half foot shorter than her partner. Dean kept his whiskey-brown hair brushed straight back from his forehead, with only a few stubborn strands hanging over one sapphire eye to graze his cheek. Everything about Agent Steelman, even the way his tie was often slightly askew, screamed *detective noir*.

Tonight, however, both Dean and Sherry had abandoned their typical office attire, as Sunday nights weren't exactly in their normal work schedules.

Agent Cowen set a handful of manila folders down in the center of the oval table, and Amelia turned her attention to the task at hand.

Spreading out the four folders, Sherry offered Amelia and Zane an apologetic smile. "Sorry to keep you guys waiting. I know we've got all these files digitized, and we can pull them up on the projector, but it sometimes helps to see everything physically laid out."

Dean chuckled as he closed the door. "You don't have to lie to us, Cowen. By now, Storm and Palmer know how much you hate fightin' with technology."

With a huff, Sherry pushed a strand of ash-blond hair from her face and rested both hands on her hips. "Two things can be true, all right?"

Zane flashed one of his trademark grins, the corners of

his gray eyes crinkling. "She's got a point, you know. There's a reason we always make murder boards." A hint of his native Jersey accent tinged his words. Considering he'd spent the first eighteen years of his life in Jersey City, Amelia figured his manner of speaking would never change.

Even though Amelia and Zane had known one another for almost a year, his smile still sent butterflies aflutter in her stomach.

With a mental shake, Amelia tucked away the lovey-dovey sentiment. As much as she enjoyed the company of these three fellow agents—especially the one by her side—they were here for a reason.

"Battles with technology aside, the call for us to come into the office sounded urgent. SSA Corsaw didn't give us much to go on, but I'm guessing these," Amelia gestured to the manila folders, "will help with that?"

As if a switch had been flipped, the room's atmosphere went from jovial to professional. Even a little grim.

Dean took a seat beside Zane, but Sherry remained standing as she pulled out her phone. "Yes. These files contain everything we have on the murders we've linked to the body just discovered south of the city earlier today." She tapped on her device. "I'm sending you everything we've got on the victim so far."

Rather than use her phone, Amelia opened her laptop. When it came to poring over case files, she preferred the easy accessibility. As the screen loaded, she turned back to Sherry. "Has today's victim been identified?"

"He has." Sherry circled around the table to the whiteboard. "Kent Manning, age twenty-nine. Middle school gym teacher in Marquette Park, but also coaches little league baseball for the same school district."

Amelia opened her most recent email, and she was promptly greeted with the warm brown eyes and smiling face of a man almost her age. His dark hair was close-cropped but still parted to one side and neatly styled. If Amelia had to guess, the kids at the middle school likely regarded him as the "cool" teacher, the one they could confide in during tough times. Hell, if she were a middle schooler, she'd feel comfortable around his kind eyes and gentle smile.

The thought squeezed at her heart. This man's body had just been found, and by the sound of it so far, the killer was connected to at least four other crimes under federal investigation.

"Manning was a probation officer before he became a teacher." Zane glanced at Amelia, then Sherry. Amelia's own quiet determination echoed in his expression.

"Right." Sherry scooped up a dry-erase marker. "His prints were on file, which made for quick identification."

Amelia didn't miss the sense of foreboding in Sherry's tone. "Are we looking into his list of parolees? Seeing if they have alibis?"

Sherry looked through a fifth folder in her hand. "Yes, we definitely want to do that."

Amelia jotted down some notes. "And what ties him to the other murders?"

Dean's chair creaked as he pushed it back and rose to his feet. "This is where it starts to get weird, and why our SSA decided we might need a little help from Organized Crime." He reached for the first of the four manila folders on the table. "All five of our victims were found in rural Illinois south of Chicago, but they were in different locations. Even different *counties*. One of the common denominators is that they're within a few hours of the city."

Sherry tapped the marker against the heel of her hand, her demeanor turning grave. "Cause of death isn't quite certain, and the time of death for all four victims before Kent was…well, not quite a shot in the dark, but close. In and of itself, that's a common thread, but the big one is that all four, no, *five* victims were found with most of their vital organs missing."

A flurry of questions sprang to mind, but Amelia settled on the most important. "Were the organs removed surgically or through predation?"

"Surgically."

Amelia nodded. "Were they the same organs for all five victims?"

Flipping open his manila folder, Dean nodded. "Lungs, liver, kidneys, heart, even parts of their intestines. The eyes of these two," he tapped the leftmost pair of folders, "were also gone, but the forensic pathologist suspected scavengers might have gotten to them. Both of those vics were badly decomposed by the time they were found."

"Other than Manning, this is the most recent vic." Sherry jabbed the end of the marker at the open file. Front and center was a glossy five-by-seven print of a man who couldn't have been much older than Kent Manning.

Amelia set aside her laptop and scooted closer to the table. "Murphy Pendleton, age thirty-two, worked as a mechanic in Wicker Park. This says he was last seen leaving work in February, and he was reported missing when he didn't show up for his shift three days in a row."

Dean's focused gaze shifted to Pendleton's file. "Yeah, he just disappeared into thin air. Credit card receipts put him at a gas station on his normal route home, but neighbors said they never saw him pull into the driveway. Pendleton's murder triggered the case being handed over to the FBI. The smaller counties where the bodies were found weren't equipped to deal."

As Zane leaned back in his chair, he tapped an index

finger against the armrest—a tell Amelia had noticed when he was contemplative. "Did all the victims live in Chicago?"

"No, not all of them." Dean flipped open the second folder in line. "Ollie Whitaker's body was found in early December. Dumped in a rural area, missing his vital organs, just like the others. He was an accountant in Peoria." The agent let out a short sigh. "Unfortunately, he'd been dead for around a month by the time he was found, so it was difficult to find useful evidence."

Amelia was about to ask if all the victims were men—a rarity for a serial killer—when Dean opened the third folder. "Maggie Hopkins. Age twenty-seven, worked in human resources for a retail store."

Maggie's light-brown eyes sparkled with youth, and even in her driver's license photo, the young woman practically radiated happiness. As Amelia moved to the next page in the file, she came face-to-face with the image of Maggie's mottled, bloated face. All the color in her cheeks had drained away, leaving the pallid flesh of a rotting corpse.

After more than two years with the FBI and ten years in the military, Amelia was no stranger to death. But even now, with all she'd witnessed, a little piece of her heart still broke when she saw how cruelly and abruptly a bright light like Maggie Hopkins could be snuffed out of existence.

Not that she ever wanted the sense of melancholy to diminish. Empathy was a vital part of her humanity, and she wouldn't lose it to desensitization. She used the feelings to motivate herself, to keep going when all hope of finding a new lead had dissipated.

Tapping the gruesome photo with the cap of the dry-erase marker, Sherry Cowen glanced from Amelia to Zane and back. "Ollie Whitaker's body was found about ten miles away from the site where Maggie Hopkins had been dumped three months earlier. Like Dean said, we weren't brought in on this case until Pendleton was found. The locals organized a search of the area around the two dump sites, but they didn't find anything."

The news didn't surprise Amelia. Though she'd been born and raised in Chicago, she'd made enough trips to rural Illinois to understand how vast the Midwestern countryside was.

She gestured to the fourth folder. "And who is this?"

Dean flipped open the case file. "The first victim we know about. We aren't ruling out the possibility that there could be more bodies that haven't been discovered." He pointed to a driver's license photo of another young woman, her honey-brown eyes no less lively than Maggie's. "Christine Fry's body was found early June of last year. Like the other four, she'd been dumped in rural Illinois. Her body was found in a creek, and even though the M.E. determined she'd only been dead for a few days, the water and the summer weather did a number on her."

Studying the woman's information, Amelia held back a sigh.

During the same month when Christine's body had been butchered and dumped, Amelia and Zane had been in the midst of a sex trafficking investigation—the same investigation that landed Amelia on the radar of not just the Leóne crime family, but a billionaire D.C. lobbyist known as The Shark.

Who would have thought her first big case at the Chicago Field Office would be so eventful?

Then again, her entire family had a penchant for landing in hot water. Amelia's older brother, Trevor, had been killed when he'd gotten too close to a corrupt senator's deep, dark secret, and her younger sister, Lainey, was a heroin addict. When Amelia's mother had succumbed to cancer twenty years ago, her father had slipped into the throes of an alcohol addiction. Though he'd been clean for four years, the damage to Amelia and her siblings during their formative years had been done.

As for Amelia? Well, her days certainly weren't devoid of their own controversy. When she'd been a sophomore in high school, she'd dated the heir to a mafia family's throne. If his father hadn't chased her out of Chicago and away from his son with lewd threats, only God knew where she'd have ended up.

Invisible spider legs skittered down Amelia's back, and she silenced the thoughts. She'd made peace with her bizarre family history. Even Zane knew about the Storms' oddities, and none of the information had changed the way he viewed her.

Amelia swept her gaze over the four photos before her attention came to rest on Dean and Sherry. "You guys have been looking at this from a serial killer angle, then, right?"

"Right." Sherry waved a hand at the photos. "There are men and women here, but there's definitely some commonalities between all the vics. They're all around the same age, healthy, and excluding Kent Manning, they were all single at the time they were killed."

Scratching the side of his unshaven face, Zane leaned back in his chair. "And their vital organs were missing."

The pieces clicked together in Amelia's head, lending the air a foreboding chill. "So we're thinking we might be dealing with an organ theft ring?"

Dean's face was a solemn mask. "That's why you guys are here. You've got a good grasp of the way organized crime operates in this city, and we could use fresh eyes. We aren't ruling out a serial, obviously, but we need to consider all our options."

All our options.

The words echoed in Amelia's head like she was standing

in a dark, dank cave. During her tenure with the Bureau's Organized Crime Division, she'd dealt with all manner of traffickers—drugs, guns, prostitution. Organ theft, on the other hand, was a bit more involved than selling a kilo of cocaine to the mob. Especially when the perpetrators were murdering their vics to harvest *all* their organs, not just drugging them to steal a kidney.

One word during the conversation stuck out to her. *Healthy.*

"But were they healthy on the inside? We need to cross-check family practitioners, surgeries. We need to start looking into medical history. Maybe our unsub knows for a fact that these vics were healthy through and through."

Whoever they were, Amelia was confident of one thing. Whoever their unsub was, they wouldn't stop until they were dead or behind bars.

3

Amelia hadn't been to the medical examiner's office in several weeks, but the sterile scent of cleaners wafting up to greet her and Dean Steelman as they approached the lower-level exam rooms was just as she remembered. During their impromptu briefing, Kent Manning's body had been en route to the Cook County M.E.'s office. As soon as Breena Ackerly had recognized the similarities to the Pendleton case, she'd stowed Manning's body away and notified the FBI.

Back at the field office, Zane and Sherry had been preparing to meet with Kent Manning's parents to ask a few routine questions, since Kent's wife was out of town. When the choice came to interviewing a grief-stricken parent or watching the forensic pathologist crack open a dead person's sternum, Amelia preferred the latter. Autopsies weren't pleasant procedures, but they weren't anywhere near as gut-wrenching as telling a mother that her child had been murdered.

Once Amelia and Dean had locked up their personal effects and pulled protective gowns over their clothes, they headed to exam room C. Attending postmortem exams wasn't a common occurrence for Amelia or most agents in Organized Crime. Recently, however, Amelia had tossed around the idea of transferring to the Violent Crimes Division. The agents in VC still didn't sit in on as many autopsies as local homicide detectives, but if Amelia wanted to move to VC, familiarizing herself with the process couldn't hurt.

Making a mental note to ask for pointers from Sherry or Dean later—preferably when they didn't have quite so many tasks on the to-do list—Amelia followed Agent Steelman into the exam room.

Clipboard in hand, the forensic pathologist greeted Amelia and Dean with a warm smile. Dr. Adam Francis's goatee was as neatly trimmed as always, and though his dark skin was only slightly lined, his facial hair sported a dash of salt.

Dr. Francis clicked his pen and set the clipboard down next to a pair of stainless-steel sinks. "Evening, Agents." He gestured to the sheet-covered body in the center of the room. "The vic just arrived about twenty minutes ago. We've got all the paperwork filled out for the transfer, so we'll start the postmortem as soon as my assistant is back."

Dean took a step toward the exam table as he peered at the covered body. "What did the county medical examiner have to say? Any estimate on the time of death yet?"

As he turned on the faucet, Dr. Francis looked over his shoulder. "Just a preliminary estimate, of course. He recorded the body's internal temperature, and based on that, it's likely the vic was killed somewhere around thirty-six to forty-eight hours ago."

One of Dean's eyebrows quirked up. "That's the freshest body we've found so far. It's been cooler than average the past couple days, so that'll hopefully work in our favor."

Amelia recalled the grotesque image of the first victim,

Christine Fry. Fry had likely only been dead a few days, but since her corpse had been dumped in June, she was even more decomposed than the victim found most recently. Murphy Pendleton had been dead for an entire week, but the cold February temperatures had left him far less decomposed than Christine Fry.

The door opened, and a young woman entered the sterile space. Her dark hair was pulled away from her face in a neat bun, and she wore burgundy scrubs under her protective gown.

"This is my assistant, Melody Novak. Ms. Novak is in her final year of medical school at the University of Chicago. She's training to become a forensic pathologist. Ms. Novak, these are Agents Amelia Storm and Dean Steelman from the FBI."

Melody smiled at Amelia and Dean. If she was intimidated by the presence of two federal agents, it didn't show. "Nice to meet you."

Amelia returned the med student's smile. "Likewise, Ms. Novak."

As Melody and Dr. Francis pulled on the rest of their protective gear and prepared the tools for the postmortem exam, Amelia and Dean moved off to the side.

The stench of decay hadn't risen to smack Amelia in the face when she first entered the room, but the sickeningly sweet scent gradually permeated her airways as if it were being pumped into the room.

The forensic pathologist pulled the white sheet away from Kent Manning's face, and Amelia reflexively turned toward the stack of barf bags near the sink. To her continued amusement, the paper baggies were adorned with a barfing emoji, just as they had been the first time Amelia and Zane sat in on one of Dr. Francis's autopsies.

Though Dr. Francis embodied every element of professionalism, the bags were a quiet reminder of the man's sense of humor. Working in such a bleak field, a person had to be able to laugh. Amelia was quite certain they'd go insane otherwise.

With Melody Novak's help, Dr. Francis moved methodically through the start of the external exam. They scraped beneath the victim's fingernails, combed through his hair, and took swabs from inside his mouth.

As Dr. Francis pulled the sheet down to the victim's waist, Amelia noted the gauze and plastic wrap around his torso. The fabric had once been white but was now stained from dark splotches of dried blood.

She hadn't been under any illusion that the dead man on the autopsy table would be unharmed, but the use of gauze was...*bizarre.*

Dr. Francis reached for a pair of scissors. "Victim's torso is wrapped in a thick layer of gauze, which is covered by plastic wrap." He glanced to Amelia. "Same as the previous victims. We'll cut off the material and bag it as evidence for analysis."

From the rundown Sherry and Dean had provided on the case so far, Amelia already knew what to expect beneath the filthy bandage, but she still craned her neck for a better view. As Dr. Francis and Melody Novak worked to carefully remove the wrap, the only sound was the slicing of the scissors and the rustle of material when the gauze and wrap fell away.

With the material removed, Amelia's attention snapped straight to the garish wound in the center of the man's chest. The decomposition had discolored what was once the deep red shade of blood and flesh. But rather than detract from its gruesome appearance, the rot only made the desecrated cartilage, muscle, and bone more macabre.

There was no shortage of coagulated blood in the victim's

chest cavity, and the stench of decay became far more potent without the wrap. However, aside from the blood and discolored tissue, Kent Manning's chest was empty.

Dr. Francis held a ruler beside the incision as Melody Novak snapped a few photos. "I conducted the autopsies of three of the other four victims. The very first victim's postmortem was done by Dr. Ackerly. Even though the states of decomposition varied between victims, they all had these identical incisions. It's very strange."

Shifting her weight from one foot to the other, Amelia exchanged a curious look with Dean, but neither of them spoke. Dean's face mirrored Amelia's thoughts. *If someone with Dr. Francis's experience is perplexed, then we're in for a ride.*

The pathologist straightened to his full height and turned to Amelia and Dean. "One other detail worth mentioning is that, at first glance here, Manning's body is clean. Very clean. There are traces of the environment where he was found, but I'm not seeing any evidence of what might have happened *before.*"

Dean tilted his head to the side, appearing thoughtful. "You're referring to defensive wounds? That's consistent with what we saw on the others."

It might've been Amelia's imagination, but she was certain Dean's West Virginian accent was less pronounced than it had been back at the field office.

"True." Dr. Francis beckoned Amelia and Dean closer before pointing to a slight bruise on Manning's neck. "But there is one thing. See this?"

Amelia took a step closer, holding her breath to avoid sucking in a lungful of decay. "Did someone punch him in the neck?"

Holding the ruler next to the abrasion, Dr. Francis paused as the shutter of Melody's camera *click-click-clicked.*

"Not quite a punch, or if it was, there wasn't much force

behind it. Enough to leave a slight bruise, which by itself gives us a little information. A person must be alive for a bruise to form, which means..." The M.E. left the thought unfinished as his eyes shifted back and forth between Amelia and Dean, almost like a teacher quizzing his students to ensure they'd been paying attention.

Amelia nodded her understanding. "It means the perp didn't kill him right away."

"Exactly. Now look a little bit to the side. See that mark?"

If Dr. Francis hadn't directed her gaze, Amelia might've missed the tiny spot. "I see it. What is it? A mark from a needle?"

"Correct. We'll run a tox screen, and..." Dr. Francis pursed his lips. "If Manning is connected to Pendleton and the others, we'll find a whole cocktail of drugs in his system."

Amelia's curiosity was piqued. Though she and Dean had discussed the case on the short drive to the M.E.'s office, they hadn't gotten to some of the nitty-gritty details. "What are some of the drugs that were found in other victims?"

Dean snorted. "A lot."

Before Amelia could ask her sarcastic colleague to elaborate, Dr. Francis chuckled. "Agent Steelman isn't wrong. We'll know more when the tests come in, but because of the number of substances we're screening for, the results will take a little longer. In Murphy Pendleton, we found substances used in general anesthesia, such as propofol and fentanyl, as well as some powerful benzodiazepines. So Manning will be screened for all of those as well."

"And those substances were found in all four other victims?"

Dr. Francis turned Manning's arm and held the ruler next to a prominent mark on the inside of the elbow. "Again, the injuries were more difficult to examine in most of the previous victims due to the states of decomposition. But based on the tox screens, and the matching injuries found on Murphy Pendleton and now on Kent Manning, we can assume the other victims were also dosed intravenously with the same or similar substances."

Amelia returned her gaze to Dean. "Properly administering general anesthesia requires training and pharmacological knowledge. Why would the perp put the victims under when he planned to kill them?"

"We're not sure. I think that depends on the type of killer we're dealing with. If he's a serial killer, then removing organs is a part of his ritual. It could be religious or symbolic. Maybe they're using the anesthetic to kill the victim."

"That could be." Dr. Francis held the ruler next to a long incision over the victim's abdomen. "Cause of death has been difficult to pinpoint so far, and some of the substances used for general anesthesia are also used in lethal injection."

"What about Christine Fry?" Amelia was hoping for a through line.

Were they dealing with organ thieves or a psychopath who fancied himself some extrajudicial executioner? The idea was disconcerting. In Organized Crime, Amelia was used to dealing with contract killers and mobsters—men and women who killed for money and revenge. Both motives were easy to understand, but serial killers and vigilantes? Lunatics propelled to commit heinous acts based on a farfetched system of beliefs? Those were mysteries to Amelia, and she wanted to understand them better.

Put yourself in the shoes of an unhinged murderer. Why would you put someone under, then take their organs?

The expertise she'd accumulated in Organized Crime made the answer obvious. Money. Sell the organs on the black market and make a bundle.

But if this was something else, money was not what motivated serial killers.

Maybe this is some lunatic trying to create Frankenstein's monster, or they're trying out mummification for the first time.

Removing each victim's vital organs fit with mummification, and the practice had just the right amount of symbolism to make it interesting for a psychopath. Amelia recalled a documentary she and Zane had watched about the belief system of ancient Egyptians. Not all the pieces fit, but there were enough commonalities to make the idea worth mentioning.

"Could the killer be mummifying the victims?"

Dean looked away from Kent Manning's body, but Dr. Francis and Melody Novak continued their work as if Amelia and Dean weren't in the room. "Mummifying? They could be. But didn't the Egyptians leave behind the person's heart so they'd have it in the afterlife?"

Amelia's first inclination was to ask how Dean knew the heart was left behind, but she brushed the thought aside. "But who's to say our killer is following the process exactly?"

The agent lifted a shoulder. "Could be. Putting someone under seems like a lot of work if all they want to do is pull out their organs and put them in jars, though."

Amelia bit back another sigh. He had a valid point. "That's true. And mummification was done out of respect for the dead, not to torture them. They honored them, not dumped them."

"Right. These bodies were discarded like a crumpled-up fast-food bag out a car window. We'll put a pin in it, though, and circle back if the case dictates it."

As Dr. Francis and Melody Novak continued the post-mortem exam, Amelia and Dean lapsed into silence, choosing instead to quietly observe the medical experts at work.

After the handful of incisions were photographed, Dr. Francis brandished a scalpel for the first time. With a long stroke of the blade, he cut all the way down to Manning's groin.

Amelia waited in silence. All she could see was gore, but if anyone could extrapolate what had happened to Kent Manning, it was Dr. Adam Francis.

He detailed each step he made for the audio record as his assistant snapped photos. Amelia listened closely, intent on understanding each step.

By the time Dr. Francis returned his attention to Amelia and Dean, his expression was grave. "Well, it's as I suspected. The incisions made to remove Mr. Manning's heart from his chest were very precise, and they were made with an equally precise tool. We couldn't quite discern the quality of the incisions in any other previous victims on account of their states of decomposition. But the precision in Mr. Manning's chest is plain to see."

The taste on Amelia's tongue turned sour. She'd dealt with a killer who liked to hack up his victims before dumping their bodies, but not one who was capable of surgically removing a person's heart. "Meaning whoever removed Manning's heart has experience in a medical field."

"That's putting it lightly." Dr. Francis gestured to the mess of discolored tissue. "Removing a human heart without damaging it isn't an easy task. And as we continue the exam, I suspect we'll find equally precise cuts where the victim's other organs have been dissected."

Shit.

Amelia kept the curse to herself. "So we're looking for a surgeon?"

Gaze shifting between Amelia and Dean, Dr. Francis nodded. "Very likely."

The concept made Amelia sick. Surgeons took an oath to "first, do no harm." But this surgeon was *harm's* very definition.

4

Zane hadn't been thrilled when Spencer Corsaw called him and Amelia into work on a Sunday evening, but as he and Sherry Cowen drove through the city to visit Kent Manning's parents, he said a quick prayer of thanks to whatever deity might've been listening for the lack of congestion on the roads.

Chicago traffic was some of the worst in the country, but on a Sunday night, the roads were bearable. Sure, he'd grown up in Jersey City, a place which wasn't exactly known for its *lack* of traffic, but even Jersey traffic paled in comparison to the everyday mess in the Windy City.

As he eased his silver Acura to a stop at a red light, Zane glanced at his passenger. "What else have we got on Manning so far?" He still wasn't quite sure what to make of the case. At this point, they could easily be searching for a serial killer or a professional organ thief.

Sherry pulled a tablet from her handbag and tapped the screen. "Not a lot so far, just what's in his missing persons file."

Zane smiled at the piece of technology. "A tablet? I thought you had an ongoing war with anything tech-related."

Sherry hugged the device to her chest. "This little beauty seems to do what I want, so I've granted it amnesty."

"Well, if things go south between you two, promise me you won't throw it at me." Zane returned his gaze to the stop light, growing serious. "Who reported Manning missing?"

"His wife. According to her statement, Kent went to the gym and didn't come home that night. She thought he might've stayed with a friend, but when he didn't come home the next day, she reported him missing. That was ten days ago."

"That's...weird." Until Megan Manning was identified as their serial killer, Zane doubted they were dealing with a domestic dispute, but with a case like this, they couldn't afford to leave any stone unturned.

"Yeah. He didn't text her back, didn't answer his phone, nothing. And she just assumed he was giving her the silent treatment, apparently. In the missing persons statement, she mentioned they'd gotten into an argument, so she thought he might've been cooling off."

Zane frowned. "Not returning home? The silent treatment? That's no way to manage an argument."

Sherry scoffed. "Wait until you and Amelia have your first real fight. You'll be afraid to come home too."

She wasn't wrong. But she wasn't right either. Zane couldn't imagine a fight with Amelia that would be bad enough for him to stay away from her that long. And he'd never given anyone the silent treatment. That was a selfish, juvenile tactic.

"I guess we won't know more until we get to talk to her." Curiosity gnawed at the back of Zane's mind as the light turned green and he pulled away from the intersection. Spouses were typically suspect number one in a homicide case, but when it came to his work in organized crime, they didn't often come across such cut-and-dried investigations. "You got ahold of Megan earlier today before the briefing, right?"

"Right. She's been visiting her sister in Maine. She left last Wednesday night, returning this coming Tuesday. When I spoke to her, she said she'd contact the airline and fly back to Chicago as soon as possible, though."

She leaves the state while her husband is missing?

Zane wasn't about to jump out of his seat to nominate Megan Manning for Wife of the Year, but at least she'd been willing to cut her vacation short. "Did Megan say why she went to Maine when her husband was missing for almost a week?"

With a quiet snort, Sherry locked the tablet and returned the device to her handbag. "The trip had already been planned. Nonrefundable plane tickets. I don't think I'll ever understand some people."

"You and me both." In fact, the more Zane mulled over the situation, the less he understood it. As he attempted to put himself in Megan Manning's shoes, he was even more befuddled.

Perhaps with Megan and Kent's marriage on the rocks, Megan simply hadn't cared that her estranged husband was missing. Zane couldn't relate, but not all human beings experienced empathy for others. Or maybe she was a compassionate person and just hated the crap out of the man she was married to.

What would he do if something happened to Amelia? Even just the thought of her going missing, of not seeing those forest-green eyes sparkle when she smiled every morning or feeling the soft warmth of her porcelain skin next to him at night...the thought was like a phantom hand clamping down around his throat.

I sure as hell wouldn't go out to Jersey to visit Mom and Tina.

If anything, Zane suspected his mother and sister would fly to Chicago to be with *him*.

In his and Amelia's line of work, each case had the potential to put their lives in danger. Hell, Amelia had already been kidnapped and almost killed by another FBI agent. But thanks to Spencer Corsaw's deadly aim, Glenn Kantowski was six feet under now.

Then, of course, there was Joseph Larson. As Larson's livelihood and freedom had been circling the drain, the crazy asshole had kidnapped Amelia's sister-in-law, Joanna, to use as bait to lure Amelia into a trap so he could exact his final revenge.

A twinge of guilt prodded Zane's heart, but he dismissed the sentiment as quickly as it formed. They'd planned the confrontation with Larson meticulously, and if Zane had been stupid enough to charge in at Amelia's side, Joanna Storm would be dead. Amelia was more than capable, and she didn't need Zane to hover over her "in case of an emergency." She'd proven over and over that she could handle herself, and though he still worried when she approached a dangerous situation, he also believed in her.

Besides, with that many enemies inside the FBI, do we really need to even worry about the suspects anymore?

Zane held back a quiet chuckle at his own bleak thoughts. Amelia was considering transferring to the Bureau's Violent Crimes Division, and Zane completely understood her motivation. Not only was she sick of being shot at by the mob, but she was sick of the mob corrupting fellow FBI agents to shoot at her when their contract killers couldn't.

"In one thousand feet, turn left."

The thick British accent of the GPS navigator drew Zane's attention back to the present. He'd been driving on autopilot while his thoughts wandered away from the Manning case.

Focus.

So far, the working theories involved either an organ thief or a deranged serial killer. Personally, Zane preferred the former over the latter. He could wrap his head around the motives of mafiosos, but serial killers were a completely different breed.

Where did Megan Manning and her bizarre behavior fit into either of their current theories?

Ostensibly, Megan's trip to Maine ruled her out as a suspect in her husband's murder. Kent's estimated time of death was currently thirty-six to forty-eight hours ago, meaning Megan was far away from the area when Kent was killed. Problem was, Kent went missing before Megan left for Maine.

What had the killer been doing with Manning for the week prior to his death? Zane shuddered to think...

He filed the thought away for later. As he pulled the car to a stop in front of a two-story Victorian, he fished a pack of gum from his pocket and popped a piece in his mouth. The burst of spearmint was a refreshing change from the faint coffee taste lingering on his tongue, and he was certain the Mannings would appreciate his foresight.

He offered a piece to Sherry, but she declined. "Gum just makes me hungry."

Zane chuckled. "I can't say I've ever heard that before."

"It's the chewing, I think." Handbag in her lap, Sherry leaned forward to examine the well-maintained Victorian. "How much do you think this place costs anyway?"

Money had never been an issue for Zane and his family. Though his mother, Anne, had abandoned her position as a hedge fund manager to start her own nonprofit to help those struggling with domestic violence, she had more money than her family would ever be able to spend in numerous lifetimes.

As a result, *cost* wasn't an aspect of life to which Zane gave much consideration. He was pointedly aware of how privileged he was, though, because his mom had raised him to be empathetic and gracious.

The family had other issues to manage for certain, but money wasn't one of them.

After a spell of silence, in which Zane pretended to study the Mannings' house and the surrounding neighborhood, he shrugged. "I've got no idea. Real estate isn't exactly my forte."

Sherry shot him a good-natured grin. "It's not mine, either, but Teddy's parents were real estate investors before they retired." She waved a dismissive hand. "It's okay, it's not important. I just didn't expect Kent Manning's parents to be loaded, since he was a probation officer turned middle school gym teacher."

"True. We'll have to keep it in mind, take a look at life insurance and all that. If Kent's parents are well-off, it stands to reason Megan might've thought she had something to gain if he was dead." Not that Zane's theory fit with an organ thief or a serial killer, but even mundane leads could take them in unexpected directions.

They got out of Zane's silver coupe.

Branches rattled overhead as a cool breeze whispered through the neighborhood. Most of the trees were still devoid of leaves, but a few sported tiny green buds. It was characteristically quiet for an upscale neighborhood on a Sunday night.

They climbed a few wide steps to a covered porch, the sides of which were lined with stone planters. Nothing sprouted from the dark earth yet, but he was sure that would change in the coming weeks.

Zane rapped his knuckles against the sturdy, wooden door and stepped back.

"Just a second." The woman's voice was muffled, but nearby.

As the door creaked open to reveal the tired face and bloodshot eyes of a dark-haired woman, Zane and Sherry produced their badges.

"I'm Special Agent Palmer, and this is my partner, Special Agent Cowen. You're Jillian Manning, correct? We spoke on the phone a little bit ago."

"Yes, of course." Jillian opened the door wider and beckoned them inside. "Come in. We can talk in the dining room."

Though the foyer was every bit as classy as the exterior of the house—sporting a cushioned bench and shoe rack along the wall to the right and a sitting area with an antique lamp and two wingback chairs to the left—the somber air negated Zane's ability to admire the space.

Less than two hours ago, Neal and Jillian Manning had been informed of their son's death. Kent had been missing for eleven days, and though Jillian and Neal had surely drawn their own macabre conclusions, receiving confirmation that their worst fears had come to life was on par with a physical blow to the head.

In silence, Zane and Sherry followed Jillian to a tastefully decorated formal dining area. As they took seats across from her, a tall man entered the room through an arched doorway. Zane could only make out part of the spacious kitchen from his vantage point, but he was certain it had the same charm as the rest of the house.

Running a hand over his bald head, Neal Manning pulled out a chair next to his wife and sat. Zane and Sherry introduced themselves for a second time as Sherry retrieved the tablet from her handbag.

Zane ignored the sensation of his stomach sinking to the

floor. Speaking with grieving families never got easier, no matter how many times he'd done it. "Mr. and Mrs. Manning, I'm so sorry for your loss. I know this is a difficult time for you, but we'd like to ask you some questions about your son, if that's okay?"

Jillian reached for a box of tissues with a trembling hand. "Yes, that's okay. If we can help in any way, we'll do whatever we can."

As Sherry pulled up a photo of Kent's lifeless face, Zane retrieved a small notepad and a pen from his jacket pocket. The Grundy County coroner, where Kent's body was found, had already identified him using the national fingerprint database. Now their focus needed to be on learning as much as they could about Kent.

"We just have a few questions we'd like to ask as we're getting started on the investigation."

Jillian and her husband exchanged a quick glance. Straightening in his chair, Neal turned his gaze to Zane and Sherry. "We'll help however we can, but could you tell us why the FBI is working our son's case, and not our local sheriff?"

On the drive to the Manning residence, Zane and Sherry had discussed how to address this potential question. At such an early stage in the investigation, they had to tread carefully. The FBI didn't have any answers for themselves, much less for the families or the press.

Fortunately, Sherry didn't miss a beat. "We can't reveal much at this stage in the investigation, but we've taken on Kent's case because it falls within our jurisdiction."

Neal's grim face told Zane he wasn't satisfied with the canned response, but he didn't appear ready to press the issue, much to Zane's relief.

Zane cleared his throat. "To start with, can either of you think of anyone who would have wanted to hurt your son?

Anyone who might've had a grudge against Kent, new or old?"

Dabbing the corners of her eyes, Jillian shook her head. "No. Kent was always nice to everyone, even when he was a probation officer. He decided to change his career and become a teacher, but it wasn't because he disliked his work. He just enjoyed working with kids, and he was really good at it. All his students loved him."

With a wistful smile, Neal rubbed his wife's shoulder. "I think he was inspired by his mom, honestly. I'm in finance, but talking about business models always put Kent to sleep."

As heartbreaking as the conversation was, Zane maintained his professionalism. "What about Kent's marriage? What can you tell us about his relationship with Megan?"

A fleeting storm cloud passed behind Neal's eyes, and Jillian let out a long sigh. "He didn't talk to me or Neal much about his marriage, but recently, we could tell something was going on. We have family dinners once a month to stay connected to Kent and Megan, but the past two months, he'd come alone. In fact, the last time we saw Megan was Christmas."

Zane scrawled a few notes, and Sherry folded her hands atop the table. "How did they act toward one another?"

Jillian pressed her lips together, appearing thoughtful. "Kind of…robotic. Kent loved that woman, but it seemed like he was being nice to her the same way he used to be nice to his sister after Neal or I caught them fighting."

As Zane and Sherry went through the remainder of their questions, Zane grew eager to get back to the FBI office and do a deep dive into Megan Manning's background.

At first blush, Megan didn't seem to meet the criteria for the psychopath who'd killed five innocent people and removed their organs, but Zane wasn't so naïve as to dismiss the possibility.

Every serial killer, psychopath, and mass murderer lived next door to someone. In the light of day, they all pretended to be normal, functional members of society.

If Megan Manning was living behind such a mask, then Zane would pull it off to expose the monster underneath.

5

S tepping away from the whiteboard, Amelia paused to observe her handiwork. Since their return from the medical examiner's office some thirty minutes ago, Amelia and Dean had been working on a murder board to find similarities between the five victims. Dean parsed through each case file, listing pertinent details for Amelia to write on the board.

Beneath each victim's photo, Amelia had written basic details like date of birth, marital and employment status, height, and so on. Once the basic information was filled out, she'd started on the more difficult part—specifics about the victims' disappearances.

As the door to the conference room creaked open, Amelia and Dean turned toward the newcomers. Zane had sent Amelia a text that they were on their way back, but he hadn't provided any insight into how the interview with Neal and Jillian Manning had gone.

Twisting the cap onto her marker, Amelia offered Sherry and Zane a wide smile. "Welcome back, guys. How'd the interview with the Mannings go?"

With a sigh, Sherry unshouldered her handbag. "Gave us more questions than answers, wouldn't you say, Palmer?"

"I would say, yes." Zane shucked off his coat and draped it over the back of an office chair. As he went on to explain Megan Manning's bizarre travel decisions and the observations made by Neal and Jillian over Christmas, Amelia's curiosity deepened.

"Well." Dean's chair creaked as he leaned back to stretch both arms above his head. "That is pretty damn suspicious. Any idea if he had a life insurance policy she might've been after?"

Sherry took her seat at the oval table. "Nothing out of the ordinary. A cursory review of Kent and Megan's finances didn't show anything spectacular, one way or the other. They're not in debt, and they're not loaded. Kent's father, Neal, is a corporate executive, and he and Jillian are doing well for themselves, but it doesn't look like they showered their son in money. Kent has a sister, but she lives in Louisiana."

Even if Sherry had told them Kent was a secret millionaire, Amelia would've had her doubts about Megan Manning being responsible for Kent's murder. "Megan works as a graphic designer, right?"

Sherry nodded. "Right."

"According to Kent Manning's postmortem exam, his organs were removed by someone with experience in performing delicate surgical procedures." Amelia gestured to Kent's photo on the whiteboard. "He's the least decomposed victim we've found so far, but the medical examiner believes the same precision was used when removing the other victims' organs."

A crease formed between Sherry's eyebrows. "Shit. We knew about the tox screens from the previous vics. They all had the same substances in their systems that operating rooms used for general anesthesia. We'd figured, based on that, that we were dealing with a suspect who had some medical experience. But we didn't think we were looking for a *surgeon.*"

"On the plus side," Zane made a show of weighing his hands, "it narrows down the suspect pool quite a bit, don't you think?"

"Oh, absolutely." Dean chuckled. "And with everything the vics went through before they died, I wouldn't rule out the possibility that our guy or gal has an accomplice. We'll get the BAU's opinion on all this. Maybe they can shed some light on what exactly this perp's goal is."

"Beyond money?" Sherry asked.

"You mean beyond more money." Amelia tossed her hands up. "Know any surgeons who can't make the mortgage? If our perp's a surgeon, there's something else driving them."

Zane scanned the whiteboard. "Maybe. But we've got to keep in mind that we might be dealing with multiple professionals. We'll need to get Cyber to review dark web activity and see if there are any organ theft rings operating around Chicago right now."

Though Amelia hoped they were searching for a lone wolf, Zane was right. Uncapping the dry-erase marker, she waved at the murder board. "While they're looking into that, I think the best thing we can do right now is try to find a common thread between our victims. Even if we're dealing with one of the cartels or another highly organized crime ring or a sole madman with an MD, they have to find their victims somewhere, right?"

Sherry lifted an eyebrow, her hazel eyes curious as they met Amelia's. "Wouldn't they turn to trafficked people as a first option? Before going through the trouble to kidnap someone and kill them, I mean."

The suggestion made sense, and Amelia hadn't dealt with enough organ theft cases to have established much familiarity in the industry. She did know, however, that it *was* an industry. A billion-dollar one at that.

"That depends."

Amelia and Sherry both turned to Zane.

Tapping an index finger against the table, he shrugged his shoulder. "When someone gets abducted and sold into trafficking, no matter the type, they aren't exactly looked after, you know? In the sex trafficking industry especially, the traffickers will give the victims drugs like heroin to get them dependent. The victims are starved and beaten, and in the case of forced-labor trafficking, they're often exposed to pesticides and other nasty chemicals."

Amelia recalled a labor trafficking operation she, Zane, and the Organized Crime Division had taken down in rural Kankakee County, Illinois. Considering the abhorrent acts that had taken place on that farm, Amelia wouldn't have been at all surprised to learn the men running the operation had decided to harvest organs from their victims.

Zane rested his hands on the table, palms down. "I can't remember the numbers exactly, but the majority of human trafficking is done for forced labor and sexual exploitation. The remainder, which is somewhere around ten percent, if I recall, falls into an 'other' category."

Amelia paced in front of the murder board. "Which includes trafficking people to harvest their organs, among other things. But our victims weren't trafficked, so to speak. They were kidnapped, drugged, and mutilated. They didn't even leave Illinois."

"Exactly." Zane touched the tip of his nose. "Traffickers, including organ harvesters, tend to turn to the most vulnerable members of the population. Immigrants, the homeless, folks like that. But not our perp. Our perp is abducting human resource managers and middle school gym teachers. Why?"

Dean frowned. "The quality of the product." He paused to make a sour face. "I feel gross referring to human beings as a product, but you get the point. It's like you said, Palmer. People who are trafficked are subjected to inhumane conditions. I can't imagine that sort of thing is kind to their insides."

Sherry cocked her head. "But if someone's buying an organ on the black market, are they likely to be asking questions about the donor's background?"

"Now, *that*," Zane shook a finger in Sherry's direction, "I can't say for sure. My hunch is that you'd want an organ in the best possible condition. That means you'd want to know if the organ came from a drug user or someone with severe health conditions. And if our perp is selling the victims' organs, it's possible he's trying to cater to a wealthier clientele. He won't want to risk losing a sale, or future sales, by harvesting a less-than-optimal product and being dishonest about the donor's health."

Though his logic made sense to Amelia, there were still a number of question marks surrounding the theory. "To be fair, I don't think there are many working-class people who can afford to buy a kidney on the dark web. I would imagine organ trafficking already caters to the very rich. So all these psychopaths just have to maintain the status quo."

With a smile, Zane shrugged. "Storm is right. We should look for a common thread between our victims. It's pretty clear that even if we're dealing with a trafficker, he's a cut above the run-of-the-mill traffickers out there."

"That's good, Palmer." Sherry returned the expression. "We'll have to keep it in mind. Nothing about this case screams 'normal' to me, so I suppose it makes sense that we wouldn't be dealing with a 'normal' organ thief either."

As Dean stretched out his arms, he swiveled his chair back toward Amelia and the whiteboard. "Which brings us back to the victims. From what Storm and I have gathered while we worked on this murder board, one big commonality is their ages. The youngest is Maggie Hopkins, who was twenty-seven. Christine Fry was just a little over twenty-eight, and then the oldest vic was Ollie Whitaker at thirty-two."

Amelia squinted at the whiteboard as if she could make the details speak to her. "It makes sense that you'd target young people who are at their healthiest. No one wants the heart of a chain-smoking seventy-year-old. I think we need to see what we can learn about their medical history."

Zane drummed his fingers. "That's a great point. We can add it to the list. What about their work? Are there any common threads between their careers?"

"Nothing." Amelia hadn't gotten around to writing down Maggie Hopkins's or Christine Fry's jobs at the time they disappeared, but she'd memorized most of the women's details. "As we all know, Kent Manning was a middle school gym teacher and former probation officer. Murphy Pendleton was a senior mechanic at a locally owned shop in Wicker Park, where he'd worked since he was twenty. Ollie Whitaker was an accountant in Peoria. Maggie Hopkins worked as a human resources manager for a retail store, and Christine Fry was a systems analyst for a bank headquartered here in Chicago."

Sherry blew out a long breath. "Sure isn't a lot of common ground there, is there? Blue-collar jobs and white-collar jobs, office positions, manual labor, sheesh. Plus, Whitaker didn't even live in Chicago. We'll need to get the BAU's opinion on that too. If the perp is a serial killer, or if they have tendencies consistent with a serial, then we'll have to figure out why one victim was in Peoria while the rest lived in Chicago."

There were already so many peculiarities about the case, Amelia was partially inclined to throw out the rule book altogether.

Zane glanced at his watch. "Megan Manning's flight gets here at eleven tomorrow morning. I can't say for sure where she fits into all this, but we'll make talking to her a priority."

"Definitely." Sherry twisted the white gold band around her ring finger, her gaze on the whiteboard. "None of this sings 'crime of passion' to me, but stranger things have happened. Until Manning's body was found, this case was sort of sitting on the back burner for Dean and me. All we had were the tox screens and some similar wounds on all four vics. We're lucky Manning's body was found before it could decompose like the others."

Returning the dry-erase marker to the holder beside the whiteboard, Amelia made her way around the table to sit beside Zane. "These murders have all been kept pretty quiet as far as the press is concerned, haven't they?"

Dean and Sherry exchanged glances, and Dean shrugged. "Not through any special precautions we've taken. The stories just weren't that sensational, I guess. The first two, Fry and Hopkins, were so decomposed that any missing organs were initially attributed to scavengers."

Sherry stretched both legs in front of herself. "They're doing the best they can with what they have, but a case this peculiar is bound to throw even the most trained folks for a loop." She waved a hand. "But anyway, if I had to guess, that's why this didn't become a media sensation. In the first few cases, 'organ theft' wasn't even considered as a possibility, and the vics weren't linked together."

If there was one aspect of law enforcement investigations the public loved, it was a serial killer. They'd be fending off reporters as soon as the Bureau held its first press conference.

Of course, after dealing with the shitstorm that followed the ridiculously high-profile investigation of former Senator Stan Young and D.C. lobbyist and billionaire Brian Kolthoff, a little press wouldn't stop Amelia.

6

As Kari meandered back toward consciousness, she was convinced she was floating. The beeps and hisses of the world around her were muffled and dull, like she was underwater, and the sounds were coming from the surface. In some of the sci-fi shows she'd watched with her ex-husband, a character would submerge themselves in a salt-water solution to deprive their senses so they could focus entirely on a certain task.

Sensory deprivation, that was what it was called. Was Kari in a tank of warm saltwater? Was that why she could barely make out the details of the world around her? Or was she dreaming? Where in the hell was she?

Focus. Think, dammit, think! What's the last thing you remember before...before...

Before what?

Just open your eyes. Move your toes. Do something.

The warm depths of sleep were tantalizing, though. Trying to decipher the world around her was...*complicated.* If she just went back to sleep, perhaps her memories would piece together her situation differently when she woke again.

That's bullshit. If you go back to sleep, you'll never figure out what's going on.

Like a teenager finally relenting to their parent's fiftieth request to wake up and get ready for school, Kari reluctantly pushed aside her desire to fall back into unconsciousness. As she swallowed, her mouth felt as if it were stuffed with dirty cotton balls. The taste on her tongue was foul, the type of morning breath she'd only ever experienced after drinking heavily at a couple of parties in college.

Was that what had happened? Had she drunk herself into a stupor and blacked out somehow? Or worse, was she in an ICU with a machine keeping her alive?

No, that wasn't right. Kari had done her share of partying in college, but as an adult, she only ever had a glass of wine or a beer when she was out with a friend or visiting her dad to watch a Bears game.

She clung to that last memory like a life preserver in an ocean. Anything to avoid slipping back to the comforting numbness of sleep. Her gut told her if she let herself drift off, she'd never come back. If her grasp on the life preserver slipped, she'd be lost to the dark depths of her own unconsciousness.

White-hot panic fizzled around the edges of her thoughts. Where the sense of dread should have overwhelmed her with a maelstrom of adrenaline, she was merely a bystander to her own plight. A person standing on a calm beach, watching lightning dance from cloud to cloud way off in the distance.

Where am I?

She didn't have an answer.

Fine. What's the last thing you remember? You weren't out getting hammered, so what were you doing?

Aside from working and visiting her dad, Kari didn't do much outside her house these days. When the weather was nice, she'd take a break from the treadmill in the basement and go for a run at a park near her house.

As quickly as a lightning bolt slamming into the ground at Kari's feet, she remembered.

The park. The kid wandering around by the creek taking pictures for his class. Then the strange man she ran into on her way back to the parking lot. The punch. The needle.

For a beat, terror jumbled her thoughts. What had been in that syringe? She'd been knocked out almost immediately, and from there...nothing. Her mind was blank.

Was she even alive? Why would a perfect stranger sedate her?

To kidnap you. Come on, you've seen the news. People go missing all the time. Remember the story about that woman who was kidnapped and held captive on some rich creep's yacht for seven months?

How could she forget? The woman's name had never been released, but the news stories had claimed she was a Chicago resident.

I don't live in Chicago anymore. I live in the suburbs. Why would someone come to the suburbs when the city's so much more convenient?

The *why* and *how* of her current situation would have to wait. For now, if Kari wanted any shot at solving this puzzle, she needed to fight her way out of the bizarre fugue clouding her brain.

Breathe in, count to four. One, two, three, four. Now try to move your fingers and toes.

Panic threaded through her tired body as she strained and concentrated, but the sentiment was short-lived. With all her strength, she managed to move her fingers. Her nails scraped against plastic, though she didn't have the first clue what the surface was. When she wiggled her toes, she permitted herself a moment of cautious optimism.

If she wasn't paralyzed, then she could fight. And if she could fight, then maybe she could get out of here. Wherever the hell *here* was.

With pitiable reserves of energy left in her body, Kari willed herself to open her eyes. The minuscule movement seemed to require Olympian-level strength.

Muted amber light filtered past her cracked lids. The persistent beep at her side was clearer, and the hum from somewhere else in the room no longer gave the illusion that she was underwater. Blinking once to clear her vision, she turned her attention to the pastel-blue blanket covering her body. The bed where she lay wasn't a normal bed, the plastic guard rails on either side more consistent with what she'd expect in a hospital.

Maybe I am in the hospital.

Hope glimmered in the background of her thoughts.

Had the lunatic from the park tried to abduct her and failed? Maybe the kid from the creek had spotted him and called 911, and now Kari was recovering in the hospital. Then the *beep, beep, beep* at her side would be a heart rate monitor, and the hum in the distance was—well, she wasn't quite sure what that was.

The moment of optimism gave her the much-needed energy to fully open her eyes, blinking away the film of sleep. Dark gray walls surrounded her, and the only sources of illumination were the dim, recessed lights that had seemed so bright a moment ago.

As she'd suspected, a metal IV stand rose on her right, a clear tube running down from a drip bag to where the needle was buried in a vein on the inside of her elbow.

So far, all her surroundings were consistent with a hospital. There were no windows, but not every hospital room had a view.

Check the other side of the room.

Swallowing against the gritty sensation in her mouth, Kari strained to turn her head to the left.

To another bed.

Tears of relief prickled the corners of her eyes as she scanned the person bundled in blankets identical to her own.

She wasn't alone. Somehow, she'd been saved from the madman who'd tried to abduct her in the parking lot, and now she was in a hospital.

She was safe.

Blinking away the moment of emotion, she refocused on the other patient. She'd been so overwhelmed with relief, she hadn't even noticed the various machines connected to the person's still form. Kari's medical knowledge was limited, but as she peered in the patient's direction—a man, as far as she could tell—she recognized a dialysis machine much like one a former coworker had needed. Coupled with the ventilation tube in his throat, the poor guy had to be on death's door.

Was she in the intensive care unit? She pondered how close she'd come to dying if she now shared a room with this guy.

Movement in the wall beside the other bed snapped her attention away from the medical contraptions. As a man emerged, Kari realized the wall wasn't a wall at all, not really. It was a wide pane of glass separating her and the sick man from an adjacent room.

Kari's vision blurred, and she blinked until the man behind the glass came into focus.

Though her limbs were still weighed down with lead, much of the fog in her brain had dissipated. Enough for her to recognize the man watching her and the other patient like they were specimens in a jar.

The man from the park. The same man who'd slammed a needle in her neck to knock her unconscious.

Terror raked its claws over Kari, but the only sound that slipped from her lips was a pitiable moan.

What should she do now? Had the man noticed her, or could she pretend to be unconscious in hopes that he'd leave her alone so she could try to figure a way out of here? She needed more time, time to figure out...something. A plan, a means to escape or bargain with her captor...

"You're awake." His voice echoed from an unseen speaker, cutting through her panicked thoughts like a scalpel.

Shit.

Should she respond to him? Ask him where she was? What he planned?

Did she even want to know?

Kari swallowed, but her voice failed her. She tried to lift her hand to rip the IV out of her arm, but hard plastic binding bit into her wrist, stopping the movement short. When she struggled to move her leg, she was met with the same result. Her ankles were bound in place.

She was trapped. A lone tear slipped from her eye, leaving a chilly trail as the drop snaked down her cheek.

An eerie smile crept onto the man's face as he strode out of view. Seconds later, a door next to the wall of glass opened. With the same unsettling expression, the man stepped over the threshold, his gaze fixed on Kari.

"There, there, Kari. Don't panic." As he moved a gloved hand out from behind his back, Kari's gaze shot straight to the syringe he held.

The cadence of the heart rate monitor beside her bed picked up speed, matching the rapid-fire drum in Kari's chest. Desperation reared its ugly head. She didn't care what she had to do—she wanted out of here. She'd beg, humiliate herself, whatever it took.

Licking her dry lips, Kari didn't let her focus drift from the needle as she struggled weakly against her binds. "Pplease..." Her voice was sandpaper gritty. "Y-you don't have to do this."

To Kari's horror, her plea only widened the sick grin on the lunatic's face.

"You'll be all right, Kari." He approached the IV stand, syringe in hand. "You'll be part of something much larger than yourself soon enough. You'll be part of *history*."

As she opened her mouth to protest, he slid the needle into the IV and pressed the plunger.

She was still forming her next sentence when her world turned black.

7

S hoving the passenger's side door open, Amelia stepped out into the abundant late-morning sunshine. Tall trees loomed on either side of the quiet street, but the lack of leaves left the sun's glow mostly unobstructed. Amelia took in a deep breath, savoring the earthy scent of spring after she and Sherry Cowen had spent forty-five minutes in traffic.

Sherry strode around the front of the car. "Not quite as ritzy as the area where Kent Manning's parents live, but they could definitely do worse."

Amelia tilted her chin at the gray stone house sandwiched between two nearly identical homes. "Not the most spacious place, but it seems like something a teacher and a graphic designer could afford."

"Agreed. Especially knowing Kent's parents could afford to help him financially."

In the eyes of an FBI agent, any and every little detail had the potential to be suspicious, even the neighborhood where a person lived. When Amelia was going about day-to-day activities like grocery shopping, she sometimes hated that she couldn't shut off the investigator part of her brain.

Better than the alternative, that's for sure.

As Amelia straightened the front of her white dress shirt, they made their way to the covered porch of the modest house. Aside from a weathered welcome mat, the space was bare.

Badge in one hand, Amelia knocked on the door with the other. Before embarking on the journey to Kent and Megan Manning's house, Sherry had called ahead to ensure Megan would be home. Though Sherry had reported that the woman seemed cooperative, the pessimistic side of Amelia still half expected to find an empty house.

To Amelia's relief, the wooden door swung inward to reveal a petite blond she immediately recognized as Megan Manning.

"Mrs. Manning, I'm Special Agent Cowen, and this is Special Agent Storm. You and I spoke on the phone a little bit ago. We have some questions for you regarding your husband, Kent Manning. Could we come in?"

Wide brown eyes flicked back and forth between Amelia and Sherry's badges. "Of…of course." Megan swallowed hard. "Come on in."

With a smile of thanks, Amelia stepped over the threshold, followed by Sherry.

"Can I get you anything to drink?" Pausing in the hall, Megan tightened her knit cardigan. "I just got back home, but I could make some coffee, if you're interested."

Amelia offered Megan a smile she hoped was reassuring. "That's all right, no need to trouble yourself. You're already dealing with a lot."

The expression Megan wore was despondent, but more than anything, the woman practically oozed nervousness. As Megan led the way to a sunny living room, Amelia caught a glimpse of the wedding photos decorating the short hall. In the pictures, Megan and Kent came across as a typical, loving couple.

That morning, Amelia had dug up as much of Megan's background as she could find. Part of her had hoped to find links to a shady past or a secret debt to the mob that might explain Megan becoming involved with an organ trafficker, but Amelia's search had come up with nothing.

After high school, Megan had spent two years at a community college where she'd graduated with an associate's degree in graphic design. From there, she'd worked in advertising for a cable company, then, more recently, for an independent book publisher. The couple's financials were stable. Hell, they'd even managed to pay off their student loans and chip away at the mortgage for the house.

If Megan had a background in the medical field, Amelia's suspicion might've been piqued. From what she'd found so far, however, Megan appeared to be incapable of the precise surgical procedure that had removed Kent's heart from his chest.

And his liver, lungs, kidneys, and sections of his small intestine.

Recalling Kent's hollowed-out chest cavity sent a foreboding chill down Amelia's spine.

"Have a seat, please. Make yourselves comfortable." Waving Amelia and Sherry to a sofa across from the television, Megan took her spot on the loveseat.

Amelia managed another polite smile as she accepted their hostess's offer. "Thank you, Mrs. Manning."

"Of course. You can call me Megan, by the way. I know I'm almost thirty, but 'Mrs. Manning' makes me feel old."

Sherry retrieved a small notebook and a pen from her handbag. "No problem. I'm sure you know why we're here today, and I'd like to tell you how sorry I am for your loss. I realize this is a difficult time for you, and I can assure you all the questions we have are strictly to help us find who's responsible for your husband's murder."

What little color remaining in Megan's cheeks vanished as the word *murder* left Sherry's lips. "So he was murdered, then? I haven't seen anything about him on the news, and you're the first ones to come talk to me since…he was found."

Well, that might be because you were in Maine when he was killed.

Amelia swallowed the snarky comment. "Yes, Kent was murdered. The FBI will be holding a press conference this afternoon. We wanted to speak with you beforehand."

Eyes glassy, Megan's gaze fell to her lap. "Okay. You…you have questions to ask me? I already gave a statement to the Chicago police when I reported Kent missing."

"We do, but they're just the standard questions." Amelia kept her tone as amiable as possible, despite her gut instinct screaming something was off in Megan's demeanor.

Megan clasped her hands together and lifted her chin, avoiding direct eye contact. "All right. I'll help as much as I can."

"Thank you, Megan. We appreciate it. We know how difficult this must be for you right now." Amelia glanced at Sherry, who cocked an eyebrow.

"To start with," Sherry began, "do you know anyone who might've wanted to hurt your husband? Anyone who may have harbored a grudge, even if it seemed like something insignificant to you?"

Jaw tightening, Megan slowly shook her head. "No. Everyone loved Kent. He is…*was* a middle school gym teacher and baseball coach. All his students loved him, and he was friends with almost all the other teachers at the school. Even here in the neighborhood, everyone liked him. We aren't close with any of the neighbors, but they'd always say hello to Kent."

It might have been Amelia's imagination, but she could have sworn she detected a hint of annoyance in Megan's tone. Perhaps jealousy because Kent was adored while she wasn't?

Amelia filed the observation away for later. "So that we can better understand every aspect of Kent's life, we need to know about your marriage. The good and the bad."

As Megan's grasp on her hands tightened, Amelia was certain she'd hit a sensitive topic. Apparently, the Mannings' life together wasn't all sunshine and rainbows.

With a sniffle, Megan snatched a tissue from the box on the coffee table. "It...wasn't perfect, I'll admit. But it wasn't bad, either, you know? We had our issues, but we were working on them. We were even going to marriage counseling, and it was helping."

Amelia offered a smile she hoped was reassuring. "I understand. Could you tell us a little more about your relationship? Were there any problems in your marriage?"

A pink flush bloomed on Megan's cheeks as her jaw tightened, but to the woman's credit, the frustration or embarrassment didn't make its way to her other features. Licking her lips, she glanced from Sherry to Amelia and then cast her glance downward before answering. "I don't see what this has to do with finding the person responsible for my husband's death. Why does the FBI need to know what my husband and I were working through in our marriage?"

Sherry held up a hand. "We don't mean any offense, nor are we insinuating that you had anything to do with what happened to your husband. These are standard questions that must be asked and answered."

"Fine." Megan heaved a sigh. "It was just the normal stuff. We've been together for quite a while, and things were just...

routine. We were looking for a way to get that spark back, you know? It's certainly not something any normal person would kill over. Besides, this is the twenty-first century. Divorce exists for a reason. If our marriage was really that rocky, I'd file for divorce. I sure as hell wouldn't kill Kent."

Megan's generalized comment told Amelia she was dangerously close to shutting down. Some defensiveness was always expected when interviewing spouses of homicide victims, but there was a subtle flippant undercurrent in Megan Manning's explanation that niggled at the back of Amelia's mind.

They ran through the remaining questions, and when broaching the subject of Megan's trip to Maine, Amelia fully expected another stock answer.

Much to her surprise, tears welled in Megan's eyes as she hung her head in shame. "That makes me a terrible person, doesn't it? I just…I just couldn't handle it. All the concerned looks from the neighbors, being alone in this house. I thought about canceling the trip, and I would've, if I hadn't been going to see my sister. But I just needed a break. A change of scenery. I had this stupid hope in the back of my head that I'd come home, and Kent would just be here, like nothing had ever happened."

Megan's grief was on point, so much so that Amelia was almost hit with a bout of empathy for her.

Almost.

Participating in a murder and experiencing regret and grief weren't mutually exclusive.

After a few more questions, Amelia and Sherry handed Megan their business cards and made their way back outside.

As Amelia settled into the passenger seat, Sherry closed the driver's side door and cocked an eyebrow. "Is it just me, or does it seem like there's something Megan isn't telling us?"

Though Amelia hadn't doubted her instincts, hearing the

sentiment echoed by an agent as tenured as Sherry gave her a sense of vindication. "No, it's not just you. She's leaving something out. Problem is, we can't say if it's going to be related to Kent's murder. We already know Megan doesn't have any medical experience, so it's doubtful she was responsible for removing her husband's organs."

Sherry tapped an index finger against the steering wheel. "Right. It appears that Kent's murder is connected to the other four. Whoever killed Kent most likely killed them as well, and I don't know that I like Megan for all five murders."

As they pulled away from the curb, Amelia cast one last glance at the modest house.

She'd put a pin in Megan Manning for now, but she doubted they were through with her.

8

The aromatic scent of the jasmine tea I had steeping awakened my senses as I entered the sunny kitchen and made my way to the granite bar counter. I hadn't intended to sleep so late, but I'd lost count of the last time I'd gotten a four-day weekend. When had I slept in on a Monday? I couldn't recall.

Until this morning, I hadn't had so much as a minute to myself. Not that I minded. My research was far more important than a few extra hours of reading, watching television, or getting a full night's sleep.

Despite my passion, I had to remember I still needed time to rest and recoup. I wasn't getting any younger, and this work—ridding myself of Kent Manning's body and acquiring Kari Hobill in the course of six hours—had made for a demanding day.

Stretching my back until I felt a light pop, I bobbed the spent tea bag in my ceramic mug a few more times before discarding the bag in the trash. I still had plenty of work to do today, but at least none of it was physical.

When I'd gone through medical school what felt like a

lifetime ago, I'd never once imagined I'd be *here*. My successes weren't loud or magnanimous, and I certainly wasn't famous, at least not in the usual sense of the term. However, I could already tell my work was destined for scientific greatness.

Humans were remarkable creatures, and with the aid of modern medicine, they could withstand the removal of some of their most vital pieces…for a time.

I wanted to know how long.

No one had ever tested the limits of human endurance like I had. There were far too many obstacles in the way, too many ethical or moral concerns for my colleagues in the field of medicine.

Not for me.

For obvious reasons, I couldn't share the outcomes of my case studies with the scientific community. Not yet. I'd be arrested and jailed by the small-minded individuals who ran the justice system.

All for what? For expending the lives of a dozen measly people? Besides, multiple lives were saved by each one I took. If anything, I was a positive force in this world. I was putting a real dent in the transplant waiting list, if anything.

You're welcome.

Those men and women hadn't been killed in any way that mattered. Their contribution to my research would live on for decades, even centuries after their deaths.

Without me, they'd have been nothing. They'd have lived and died as nobodies.

Someday, my work will have immortalized them, as well as me. I couldn't share my research while I was alive, but after I was gone, my devotion to the scientific community would never be forgotten. The next generation of doctors and researchers would turn to my work, and it would become pivotal to advancements in their fields.

As I lifted the mug of steaming tea, I smiled to myself. I had plenty of time left on this planet, and I'd make it count.

Warm beverage in hand, I strolled out of the kitchen to the adjacent dining area, where I'd already set up my laptop. Navigating the dark web to find buyers for my very specific *merchandise* was my least favorite aspect of the work. As much as I tried to keep the auction style listings for each organ as succinct and straightforward as possible, there were always people in the peanut gallery trying to overcomplicate the sale.

For God's sake, I was a medical doctor. If I gave these jackasses a piece of advice, such as telling them the heart of a full-grown man wouldn't fit into the chest of their dying ten-year-old son, they'd be best suited to shut up and move on. Just because this was the black market didn't mean I could ignore the basic rules of biology.

Taking my seat, I couldn't hold in a sigh.

Patience. Without the profit from these sales, I couldn't keep doing what I do. Maintaining all that medical equipment is expensive.

I turned to my potted cactus situated in front of the picture window at my side.

"It's just a means to an end, isn't it, Spike? Every great researcher needs funding for their experiments, and mine is no different. I just have to go about securing those funds in a…more creative way."

After stretching out my arms, I pulled up a specialized browser designed to route my activity in such a way that tracing my location was incredibly difficult. I realized there were no absolutes in the cyber world, but browsers like the one I used were as close as anyone could hope to get.

As I navigated to the series of listings I'd created the day before, I noted with satisfaction the number of responses I'd already received for Kari Hobill's heart and lungs.

"You're going to make me a lot of money, my dear." I didn't care all that much about financial gains, but more money meant better research.

Though Kari was ordinary in most regards, there was one aspect about her I'd known right away would draw a crowd —her size. Kari was barely four-foot-eleven, and her petite frame was as delicate as a child's.

I spared another look at Spike. "You can't take an adult human heart and transplant it into a ten-year-old. Not unless that adult is abnormally small."

People across the planet would pay good money to prolong their own lives when the organ transplant system failed them, but they'd pay exorbitant amounts to save their children. Even moral, law-abiding citizens would stoop to the level of a criminal if it meant sparing their son or daughter's life.

Coupled with Kari's universal O-negative blood type, she was a gold mine.

"No, she's better than a gold mine," I muttered to my cactus friend as I sifted through the most recent bids for her kidneys.

I always started small.

Not only was the method conducive to making more money, but it was exactly what my research required. Chip away at a person's vitality and observe their state of decline. With the dialysis machine and ventilation system I'd purchased with the profits from my first set of sales, I could keep a human being alive for as long as it took for my buyers to travel to Illinois.

I didn't just prevent my benefactors from dying. I dosed them with drugs to mitigate the body's stress responses, keeping them as docile as possible. Stress, especially the type that came with being forcibly relocated to a foreign environment, took a hefty toll on the human body. If I wanted top dollar for my subjects' organs, it was in my best interest to keep them pristine.

Of course, my plans didn't always go smoothly. Humans were unpredictable animals, and even though my intent was to keep them alive and healthy, their inclination to fight back occasionally led to…unfortunate consequences.

I held back a groan. If I ever had to clean up that much blood again, I'd be tempted to sell the equipment and set the place on fire instead.

My goal wasn't to subject my patients to excessive suffering, but when they got the bright idea to fight me, they sealed their own fates. It had been almost a year since a subject had attempted an escape. How that woman had powered through the drugs in her system would forever be a mystery. But much to my chagrin, she had.

Maybe someday, I'd find another who had her same tenacity. A subject who could withstand more than a test of resilience and overcome the basic laws of medicine. Though it had only led to monumental suffering in the end, it was something to behold. She'd had the exact amount of lidocaine in her system for such a procedure. I should've been able to remove her brain without a flinch, yet she was up and running, searching for an escape route.

The pronounced rattle of my cell vibrating against the wooden table jerked my attention back to the moment.

"Who the hell?"

Clenching my jaw, I scooped up the device.

My good spirits sank to the floor. It was my colleague.

Why are you calling me on my day off?

I considered declining the call. I couldn't say why he was calling, but chances were, it wasn't good. Either he wanted me to give up my day off and come into the clinic, or…

Mentally, I crossed my fingers, hoping he simply needed

clarification on one of our patient's files. I needed this job to maintain appearances, but it routinely drove me insane.

I gritted my teeth, took in a breath, and swiped the answer key. "Hello?"

"Good morning. Look, I'm sorry about the timing. I hope I didn't interrupt anything."

Rolling my eyes, I leaned back in my chair. "It's no problem at all. What can I help with?"

"I'm really sorry to do this to you, but do you think you could cut your scheduled break short and come in tomorrow? We've had some last-minute appointments booked, and we could really use your help."

I massaged my temple with my free hand. There was still plenty of work to be done, not just for Kari's sales, but for my other patient's sales as well. He was nearing the end, and the financial part of the transaction for his heart would be finalized soon—plenty of time before my client arrived in the city in a few days. Still...I needed to keep up appearances.

"Sure, I can do that."

"Thank you. You're a lifesaver."

This was an unfortunate development, but the tasks for the next few days weren't impossible. Kari wasn't going anywhere, and I could easily postpone the first sale of her kidney. I might even get more money from the auction if I let it run longer.

Yes, going to work tomorrow was no problem at all. It might make me more money in the long run.

Most importantly, it would give me more time with Kari. She could turn out to be instrumental in my research.

Does size really matter?

As my smallest benefactor, I was about to find out. Would she be able to hold a conversation with her liver in a jar of ViaSpan solution next to her heart monitor? With both kidneys on first-class flights to opposite coasts? One day, would I be able to watch my subjects connive and beg to be set free, not realizing their lungs were on ice two rooms over? This research was all so divine, with potentially big payouts beyond most people's wildest imaginations.

My collection of freshly sterilized surgical tools glistened under the lights of my dining room chandelier. I'd removed the instruments from my autoclave just this morning. A smile played at the corner of my mouth as I rolled up the instruments in the towel they rested on.

Time to test the boundaries of human endurance.

9

_____

As Zane took a sip from a fresh mug of coffee, he said a silent thank-you to Journey and Michelle for the new coffee maker they'd gifted before departing to Pennsylvania. Lord only knew how many calories he'd saved by cutting back on his trips to the café down the street. He missed the fancy lattes, but he doubted his blood sugar felt the same way.

Shouldering open the door to the incident room, he was pleasantly surprised to spot Agent Layton Redker seated across from Dean. Like always, Layton's dark hair was styled in a toned-down faux hawk, which only added to his youthful appearance.

Zane still didn't know how old the man was, but with a grown daughter, he had to be in his forties, maybe even his fifties. Hints of silver were visible around his ears and the short stubble on his face, but oddly enough, the gray didn't age him much.

Layton wasn't due to meet with them for another fifteen minutes, but with the seconds ticking away, Zane was glad for the BAU agent's eagerness to dive into the case.

"Morning, Redker." Zane eased the door closed. "I got a text from Agent Storm. She and Agent Cowen just left Megan Manning's house, so they won't be back at the office for another forty-five minutes or so. Traffic, you know?"

The corners of Layton's brown eyes crinkled as he grinned. "Oh, I do. I've lived in this city for almost my entire life. I don't even want to know how much of it's been spent sitting in a car."

Zane chuckled as he took a seat beside Dean. "No, you probably don't. Good to see you back in action, though. How's the healing coming along?"

Layton patted his side where he'd been shot a little more than two months earlier. Memories of pressing bloodstained towels against Layton's stomach while Amelia desperately tried to reason with the shooter still spiked Zane's anxiety.

The entire scenario had been balanced on a razor's edge. One wrong move, and they'd have all tumbled into the abyss.

"Almost good as new. Still doing some physical therapy once a week, but the doctors say I'll be back to one hundred percent within another month or so."

Zane shot Layton an approving smile. "That's good to hear. You're already familiar with our case, then, yeah?"

"Sure am." Layton had transferred from Cyber to the BAU a few months previous and always added valuable insight to their cases. He pushed open his laptop, the white glow of the screen reflecting briefly in the lenses of his glasses.

Dean leaned back in his chair. "We're facing the age-old question of whether we're dealing with a serial killer or a trafficker. Or both, God forbid."

It wouldn't be the first time they'd encountered such a phenomenon. A city the size of Chicago bred all types of lunatics. With the sheer number of humans virtually stacked on top of one another at the foot of Lake Michigan, it was no real surprise that the FBI never truly knew what it would be dealing with next.

Layton reached for a remote, and the overhead projector whirred to life. "I'm sure you don't want to hear this, but in my opinion, it could go either way. When you get down to it, there are enough surface similarities between traffickers and serials to make it confusing at first."

The observation wasn't what Zane wanted to hear, but the man was right. "Well, we've got five bodies so far, none of which had much, if any, trace evidence left behind. Not on the gauze and plastic wrap holding their chest cavities closed, not on their bodies or under their nails. Nothing aside from the debris and dirt that transferred onto their bodies from the various dump sites."

Layton pressed a button, and a map of Illinois and the surrounding states lit up the whiteboard. "Speaking of dump sites, that's where I looked first. I wanted to see if there was a definitive pattern that might help us pin down the suspect's location."

One of Dean's eyebrows lifted, his expression curious. "And?"

Zooming in on Illinois and Chicago, Layton tapped another key. Five red dots appeared on the map. "These are the locations where all our victims were discovered. Christine Fry, the victim who was found in June, was discovered right along the northern border of Livingston County. Then, Maggie Hopkins and Ollie Whitaker were both found in LaSalle County. Murphy Pendleton was dumped around the center of Grundy County, and then Kent was found along the northern border of Grundy County. See a pattern?"

As Zane followed the dots in chronological order, from the oldest to the most recent, he realized the victims were closing in on Chicago.

"They're getting closer to the city." Dean took the words right out of Zane's brain.

"Exactly." Layton circled the cursor around the northern-most dot. "I think this means he's getting more comfortable. Four of our five victims so far lived and worked in Chicago, so based on that, along with the pattern we're seeing with the dump sites, I think he's most likely based in Chicago as well. Serial killers get cockier with each kill that goes unsolved and, oftentimes, that means their dump sites start to get closer to home."

The reasoning was sound to Zane, provided they were dealing with a serial killer and not a trafficking organization. "All right. That makes sense. What about the state of the bodies? The organ removal? What's your take on that?"

Layton pressed his lips together, appearing contemplative. "It's...not the first case like this I've seen. Well, not completely. Remember Dan Gifford, the Fox Creek Butcher? He essentially conducted a novice autopsy on the men and women whose bodies he dumped, but he also cut them into pieces for disposal purposes. It was a combination of practicality and the urges that drove him to do what he did."

Zane sensed an underlying caveat to Layton's explanation. "But?"

The agent steepled his fingers. "But this suspect is different. Dan Gifford had some familiarity with the medical field, but according to the forensic pathologist's report on our current victims, the person who removed Kent Manning's organs did so with surgical precision. Not even Dan Gifford would've been capable of this."

Dean reached for a mint. "Plus, there're all the drugs found in the victims' blood and tissue samples. All five vics were given general anesthesia before they were killed."

Layton's gaze shifted to Zane. "That's where Organized

Crime comes in, right? To determine if we're dealing with an organ trafficker?"

"Right." Admittedly, Zane's first assumption about the unsub was that they were dealing with a trafficker of some stripe. The more he'd discussed the case with Agents Steelman and Cowen, the less sure he became of his first impression. As far as he could tell, their suspect could go either way.

Rubbing his chin, Layton glanced at the map and then back to Zane and Dean. "Either the suspect is putting the victims under to remove their organs to satisfy an urge, or he's got a purpose for them. It could be that he's selling them, but it's also possible he's eating them."

A jolt of surprise zipped through Zane's body. "A cannibal?"

Layton shrugged. "It's rare, but it's possible. With all the effort and precision this guy is putting into these victims, I think cannibalism is probably the least likely scenario. If he's using general anesthesia, he must have a setup that's close to hospital-grade, which wouldn't be cheap."

"If he's selling the organs, money wouldn't be an issue. There're thirty-nine organs from just our five vics." Zane did the math—it was in the millions.

"True." Dean crossed his arms. "He wouldn't waste all that time when he could just butcher them like cattle. Plus, if he's eating these people, he's letting a hell of a lot of them go to waste."

Zane ignored the unease simmering in his gut. He'd seen his share of horror during his tenure with the FBI and the CIA, but eating people wasn't anywhere on the list. Searching for a cannibal serial killer would be a new endeavor for him.

Is it weird to prefer the mob?

Fortunately, they were more likely searching for an organized trafficking operation. "All right, I think it's safe to say that no matter what, we're looking for someone who's financially well-off and who has medical experience, right?"

Layton nodded. "Both of those attributes could easily be found in an organ trafficker. There are many different types of organ trafficking, but by far the most common is what's referred to as 'transplant tourism.' Typically, that's when a person in need of a transplant, usually a kidney, travels to a developing country that has hospitals capable of performing the transplant. They'll buy the kidney from an organ broker, and the broker almost always preys on the impoverished population to fulfill the order."

As Dean's frown deepened, Zane suspected the man was going through the same line of thought he'd just experienced moments ago. He knew organ traffickers and the mob were out of Dean's comfort zone, just as cannibals and serial killers were out of Zane's.

"Most of the time, the so-called 'donor' receives payment for their kidney, but it's always a pittance of the one- to two-hundred grand the recipient pays. Hell, in Iran, it's even legal to sell your kidney." Zane waved a dismissive hand. "Anyway, we're not dealing with a classic case of transplant tourism, but it's still possible we're dealing with a form of it. If there are patients receiving these organs, they'd almost definitely have to travel to Chicago."

"True." Layton minimized the map and pulled up an organ transplant web page. "I did a little research on organ trafficking. Human hearts can only survive outside the body for a maximum of six hours. So if our unsub is selling the victims' hearts, then the operations almost *have* to be occurring within some type of medical facility in Chicago. Maybe Milwaukee, but that's a stretch. It's got to be somewhere close by with a large, well-equipped hospital."

Like so many forms of human trafficking, Zane knew

illegal transplants occurred every day, right under their noses. "If the perp knows the right palms to grease, it's something he could easily get away with undetected. That's the thing about organ trafficking. It's difficult to pin down because of its secretive nature. Now, some organ traffickers are simply affiliated with an employee of an organ retrieval service, and they obtain organs from people who are already dead. Trying to differentiate those cases from a case like ours is difficult."

After smothering it in fingerprints, Dean finally popped the mint into his mouth. "All right, here's the burning question. Which criminal organizations deal in organ trafficking? All of them?"

"No, not all of them." Thank God. "I've only been in Chicago for about a year, but I've got enough experience with the Italians to rule them out. Neither the Leónes nor the D'Amatos stick their noses in organ theft. Around here, we'd be looking for one of the bigger, more organized operations. One of the cartels, maybe, or the Russians."

Everything always circles back to the Russians.

Zane absentmindedly rubbed the edge of his collarbone—the site of a faded nautical star tattoo. The star, along with its counterpart on his other shoulder, was a symbol of authority in the Russian mob. The stars had to be earned, and with the Russians, there was only one way to earn clout—bloodshed.

Dropping his hand away, Zane forced his attention back to the incident room. The prospect that they might be dealing with the Russian mob had occurred to him before now, but he hadn't voiced the concern, not even to himself.

He hoped they weren't dealing with the Russians. He was barely a month removed from witnessing the sheer brutality they were capable of inflicting on those who crossed them. Brian Kolthoff found dead in his cell—his tongue excised and his throat sliced—was a stark reminder.

Hell, Kolthoff hadn't even snitched on the Russians—they'd killed him preemptively, and their casual viciousness toward a powerful billionaire had served as a pointed message to anyone who might have thought about getting on their bad side.

No one, absolutely *no one*, was safe from the retaliation of the Russian mob.

Not a billionaire D.C. lobbyist, not a poor girl trying to escape a trafficking ring, and not a former CIA agent trying to live out his life away from all the horrors he'd endured in that frigid Siberian hellscape.

Despite the pounding in his ears and the clamminess of his hands, Zane returned his focus to Dean and Layton.

This is not the time, Palmer. Get it together. We're probably not even after the Russians, all right? Besides, they'd have to know where you are and who *you are, and they don't, all right?*

Invisible spider legs skittered along his back.

Painting a contemplative look on his face, he hoped his colleagues would simply assume his silence was the result of a mental brainstorm, not a borderline panic attack.

Finally, when he was confident he could speak without his voice being fraught with nervous undertones, he patted the table. "Let me do a little digging, and I'll see what I can turn up about organ trafficking here in Chicago."

Layton powered off the projector. "I'll go pay a visit to some of my friends in Cyber Crimes and see about combing through the dark web to find any activity that might belong to our perp."

The new direction for their investigation gave Zane a much-needed shot of normalcy.

No one in the Russian mob was going to trace him to the Chicago FBI Field Office. If his identity had been compromised in a leak or any other manner, the CIA would have notified him.

The Agency had protocols for information breaches, and odds were, the Russian mob wouldn't waste the resources to track him down so many years after the fact. They had nothing to gain by killing him. All they'd accomplish would be pissing off the CIA, which he sincerely doubted they wanted to do.

Everything will be fine. Talk to Amelia, get her opinion, and see if she can reach out to her confidential informant to see if he might know who we're dealing with.

No matter how many times Zane reassured himself, the sliver of impending doom remained lodged firmly in the back of his head.

10

Double-checking the connection of his new webcam, Bogdan took a seat in his leather office chair and scooted closer to the pair of monitors on one side of his L-shaped desk. A slat of dull, gray light pierced through the slight gap between the blackout curtains on the south-facing window, but he didn't mind. He preferred to have at least *some* view of the outdoors, even just a sliver. Working in a dim room all day, he was strangely comforted by knowing there was a world outside his home office.

Bogdan rubbed his cold hands together and blew on them. That was what he got for fiddling around with wires for almost an hour. Even though he was in a third-story apartment, the frigid Russian air found a way inside when a man lived this far north.

He missed his home city of Saint Petersburg. It was far from being considered a tropical destination, but it beat the frigid, landlocked Yakutsk. Bogdan had spent the entire winter in the coldest city in the world.

Fortunately, the cold weather would soon abate, and

warm temperatures would thaw the nearby Lena River and make outdoor activities possible for a short period of time.

By then, Bogdan hoped to be gone.

Straightening in his chair, he opened a secure video call application he'd begun using more than a year ago. The app worked similarly to the anonymous browsers he utilized to access the dark web, and he'd been assured by his soon-to-be business partner that the signal was secure.

As the clock ticked over to eight a.m., he scrolled through his list of contacts, selected his friend's name, and pressed enter to initiate the voice call.

His friend.

A small smile tugged at Bogdan's lips. Truly, he could call the man friend, couldn't he? What had started as a casual late-night online discussion had now spanned almost a year and a half.

The soft hum of the dial tone clicked over as a familiar face populated part of the screen.

Bogdan flashed the man a grin. "Hello, my friend. How has your day been?"

Doc returned the smile. "It's been a busy one, but nothing I can't handle. How's your newest project coming along?"

"It is good. Nearly done. I will finish filming this morning after our call." Being able to talk so openly about his work brought Bogdan more joy than he'd have thought. Snuff films weren't exactly the type of topic one could broach with just any friend.

Macabre fascination glinted in Doc's eyes. "What do you have planned for the grand finale?"

Leaning back in the chair, Bogdan scratched his unshaven cheek as he mulled over the words. "I have not decided. I have thought about doing a video series that is…how do you say…*themed*. Kills based on seven deadly sins or on old folklore. I think this would draw more viewers, yes?"

Doc snickered. "Yes, I think it would. You're very creative, my friend. I think our joint business venture is going to be lucrative."

Bogdan's mood grew lighter. Though he had a substantial sum of money stashed away from producing snuff films for the last five years, more money was always welcome. Plus, the larger the audience, the larger Bogdan's influence would become.

When he added Doc's special expertise, the sky was the limit. "I think that the audience will be delighted to see what you have to offer. Science is its own form of art, is it not?"

"I suppose so. You know, yesterday, I was just thinking about how it was a shame I wouldn't be able to share any of my work until I'm gone. But truly, this," he gestured to the camera, then to himself, "is a brilliant solution to my problem. Who knows? I could even inspire other like-minded researchers to begin their own experiments. I'm very much looking forward to meeting you in person soon."

A wave of hopefulness washed over Bogdan, and for a beat, he felt like a child again. Even if he tried, he doubted he could have wiped the smile from his face. "I am looking forward to leaving Yakutsk. I did some research, and the climate of Chicago is much more appealing. Plus, some of my...*projects* seem to have attracted attention around this area. Yakutsk is home to three hundred thousand people, but the number is not so big right now."

Doc's expression sobered. "Are the authorities onto you?"

Bogdan shook his head, a hint of the doctor's anxiety shooting through him like a dose of heroin. "No, they are not onto me. They seem to think something is amiss, but they do not know who they are searching for."

Doc's shoulders relaxed, tentative relief in his gaze. "That's good."

Bogdan fought the urge to squirm in his seat. "It is good,

yes. But in Russia, the authorities are not the ones to be concerned about. You see, Russia is…different than America. The authorities are in charge only on paper. The *real* authorities are what you call the mob."

Both the doctor's eyebrows shot up in surprise. "The Russian mob?"

"Yes, exactly." Bogdan held up a hand to allay his friend's mounting concern. "I am not one of them, don't worry. My work is done separately. I handle the business by myself. Those greedy bastards would take at least half of my profits if I worked with them."

As Doc laughed, Bogdan let go of a portion of his paranoia.

The truth about Bogdan's relationship with the Russian mob was far more complicated, and he wasn't inclined to go into detail on a video call. His flight to America wasn't scheduled yet, but he and Doc had planned to meet in the near future. When Bogdan was safe in America, he could reveal his family's sordid history with the Russian mob. As long as the mob was a real and present danger to his welfare, however, he preferred not to travel down memory lane.

"If they'd take half your profits, then it sounds like you're better off on your own."

Bogdan shot Doc another smirk. "Of course. Just as you are, my friend. And when I am in America, that will not change. We will split the profits from videos of your patients, but otherwise, we will each maintain full control over our own businesses."

"I'm looking forward to it. The patient I acquired a few days ago will make me a lot of money. She's petite, which means her organs are small enough to transplant into a preteen. I tell you, people are already willing to pay top dollar to save themselves, but when it comes to their kids, you can almost double the usual price."

To Bogdan, the prospect was intriguing. "Why not harvest organs from younger children?"

For a moment, Doc appeared as if he'd bitten into a lemon. "Kids are...volatile. Unpredictable. Overall, they're just riskier to deal with than adults. If someone's kid goes missing, they're liable to burn the city down trying to find them. But if an average adult with no children goes missing? Well, the response isn't quite as raucous. I try to locate individuals who aren't married, but I won't rule them out if they are. But I never go after parents."

The explanation made some sense, but Bogdan could tell the doctor hadn't given the idea much thought. "What about runaways? Would younger children who have run away from home not be the ideal candidates?"

Silence settled over them as the doctor's face turned thoughtful. "You know, you might be onto something there. I typically prefer patients who are in exceptional physical health, but most preteen kids, even if they're runaways, are still in decent enough health. With my desire to test human endurance, I wonder if young runaways might be feistier. And with the extra money I make from selling their smaller organs, I could afford to keep them longer to ensure their health and run the proper tests to match them with suitable recipients. And expand my research in the long run."

Bogdan's grin was back. "See? Our partnership is already paying off. Teenagers are a common request in snuff films, as well, and they can be easier to trick and manipulate than adults. I will show you what I have learned once I am in America."

Returning the expression, Doc rubbed his hands together. "Perfect. In the meantime, I'll do some research of my own. We have great things ahead of us, my friend."

After a short discussion about the weather in their

respective locales, Bogdan bade his friend farewell and ended the video call.

He could hardly believe his goal of traveling to America was finally on the cusp of becoming a reality.

"I did it, brother." Bogdan spoke the words in English, even though his brother had spoken little of the language when he was alive.

As always, silence greeted him. Rurik should have been here to celebrate this moment with him and enjoy the financial gains Bogdan had made over the past half decade.

With a weary sigh, Bogdan reached down to the bottom drawer of his desk and pulled out a copy of *Moby Dick*.

He didn't like the book. Never had. It was stuffy and boring, and the damn thing kept going and going like a record stuck on repeat. But reading and rereading the text had helped him learn English as a teenager. Back when Bogdan was a kid, Rurik would sometimes give him books he'd stolen from the public library back home in Saint Petersburg.

Sometimes, when the weather was especially cold, Bogdan and Rurik would hide out in the library until after it closed. Then they'd sleep on the floor in the comic book section. Back then, only a few years after the fall of the Soviet Union, libraries in Russia had more variety—not much, but it was an improvement over the restricted media that had been allowed through the Iron Curtain.

How many years ago had Rurik given Bogdan this hardcover copy of *Moby Dick*? Twenty? Twenty-five?

Bogdan couldn't remember. Rurik had known how much Bogdan liked to read and draw, and when he'd given him *Moby Dick*, Bogdan had been elated. It was the thought that counted, after all. Now, despite his disdain for the writing itself, the book was his most prized possession.

He smiled to himself as he let his fingers skim the rough

fabric along the spine, but the good humor died the instant he flipped open the cover.

Tucked into the jacket of the book, he pulled out a worn photo taken back during his and Rurik's time at the Sea of Okhotsk. The colorful lights of a Christmas tree twinkled in the background as the brothers grinned for the camera.

But Bogdan's attention was fixed on the man standing beside the little pine tree. A man he hadn't seen in person since he'd watched him murder his brother ten years ago— little more than a year after the photo had been taken.

Mug in one hand, a cigarette in the other, the man's eyes were fixed on a point off-camera, likely another one of the men who'd been in the cabin at the time.

"Mischa Bukov." The name rumbled from Bogdan's throat like a growl. "I do not think that is your real name, though, is it?"

The photo didn't respond, but Bogdan didn't need it to. For the past eight years, he'd been convinced Mischa wasn't who he claimed to be. He'd kept a bead on the man as well as he could, considering Mischa's position of authority in the *Bratva*. Once Mischa moved to Moscow, however, Bogdan had lost track of him.

Just because he no longer kept tabs on Mischa didn't mean he'd forgotten. There was no doubt in Bogdan's mind that Mischa was an operative in either the American CIA or FBI, or possibly the British MI6, but he doubted the Brits' involvement. He wasn't under the illusion he could present that information to the Bratva and remain unscathed. Rurik's attempt to overthrow Mischa's command had landed their family name on the Bratva's shit list. Chances were, if Bogdan attempted to reveal his suspicions to a Bratva commander, he'd simply be shot and his body would be tossed in the Lena River, never to be seen again.

"I will prove them wrong, brother. I have not forgotten.

Once I am in America, I will find Mischa. I will find out who he really is, and I will make him pay for what he did to you. I will clear our family's name with the Bratva, and I will do it with Mischa Bukov's blood."

11

As a temperate breeze whispered through the small parking lot, Amelia noted the telltale scents of spring —fresh-cut grass and damp earth. Soon, blooming flowers would join them, and Amelia would have to remember to carry an entire box of tissues around with her in case she caught a whiff of the wrong type of pollen and lapsed into a sneezing fit.

The allergies only plagued her in the first few weeks of spring, thankfully. Once the weather warmed and the leaves on the trees finished sprouting, her sinuses went back to normal.

For what wasn't the first time, she wondered if a move to the tundra would be wise. Zane had expressed his disdain for the Midwest's unpredictable climate, so chances were good he'd be happy to accompany her.

Maybe a transfer to the field office in Anchorage is warranted.

The quiet crunch of tires against concrete drew her from her musings to an approaching Infiniti. Usually, Alex Passarelli beat her to their meetings at Adams Park. Today was a first.

As Alex parked the Infiniti beside Amelia's black BMW, she offered him a quick smile and a wave. Returning the gesture, he killed the engine, pushed open the driver's side door, and stepped out into the spotty sunshine.

"Morning, Alex. How was the drive?"

He rolled his shoulders and stretched his back. "Could've been worse."

"True." Amelia gestured to a nearby gazebo—the usual location of their meetings. She wasn't keen on sitting after being cooped up in the car, but she also didn't want to discuss potentially sensitive information in the parking lot. "After you."

In silence, they made their way to the quaint structure, the spring breeze following on their heels. Other than the distant specks of a couple walking a trail along the sprawling lake at the bottom of the hill, Amelia didn't spot any other occupants nearby. Nine on a weekday morning wasn't prime time for visiting the park.

Taking a seat across from Alex, Amelia expected to see his figurative shroud of unease. After all, he was a commander in the D'Amato crime family, and Amelia was a special agent with the FBI. Considering their respective professions, they should have been at one another's throats.

But as Amelia had learned when they'd dated back in high school, the world wasn't black-and-white. Alex was a mob boss, sure, but he wasn't a bad person. He'd steered his family's business to less bloody activities. And he and his fiancée hadn't hesitated to take in Mae Young. That little girl had been the product of corrupt senator Stan Young raping Alex's younger sister, Gianna. Plenty of others would've been content to leave Mae to the care of the state. But not Alex.

Amelia cleared her throat. "I guess we should cover business first, huh?"

Curiosity was plain on Alex's face. "I guess so. You need my help with something?"

"Yeah. Nothing all that specific. I just wanted to pick your brain. A case I'm working." She held back the part about Zane suggesting she reach out to Alex. He was already jumpy enough about conversing with an FBI agent, and she didn't want to make him any more skittish.

Alex visibly relaxed at the reassurance, and his obvious relief even made Amelia less tense. "All right. What've you got?"

"What do you know about organ trafficking?"

Blinking a few times, Alex shrugged. "That's...pretty far out of my wheelhouse."

Amelia wasn't surprised. "Do you know which groups deal in organ trafficking?"

Alex rubbed his chin. "Not us, that's for sure. And not the Leónes. Even just the logistics of organ trafficking is complicated. I've heard rumors that the San Luis Cartel dabbles in it, but from what I understand, most of the activity takes place on Mexican soil. Not that I'd rule them out. If there's an industry they can profit from, they'll give it a shot. Then there's the Russians."

"Right. The Russians are on our short list. This trafficking operation, if that's what it is, it's...different. The victims aren't who you'd expect to see when dealing with a trafficker." Though she trusted Alex to be discreet, Amelia didn't want to give away more information about their case than was necessary.

"That's hard to say, then. If an established criminal organization deals in organ trafficking, then they'll have a set way of going about things, you know? They wouldn't deviate from what they already know is successful."

He had a point. If the San Luis Cartel had a good track record of kidnapping homeless folks, runaways, or prostitutes and selling their organs on the black market, they wouldn't suddenly turn their sights on a middle school teacher or a senior mechanic from Wicker Park.

Ultimately, the knowledge only gave Amelia more questions than answers. Could they be dealing with an organ trafficker operating solo? Or were they truly searching for a deranged serial killer?

Blowing out a sigh, Amelia slumped back against the gazebo bench. "That's true. I hate to ask this, but could you keep an ear out?"

"It's no problem. If I hear anything, I'll let you know."

"That would be immensely helpful, thank you." She paused for a beat before posing her next question. "How's Mae?"

A ghost of a smile passed over Alex's face. "Good, actually. She's still adjusting, but she and Liliana are like this." He crossed his middle and index fingers. "She's a smart kid, and she's resilient. We'll tell her the full story when she gets older and can process it, but for now, she's just happy, like a normal kid. We enrolled her in the same school I went to, and she's been excited to make new friends."

The news lifted Amelia's mood. "That's good to hear. Kids really are more resilient than adults give them credit for. Have you and Liliana settled on a date for your wedding? I bet Mae would love to be your flower girl."

Alex laughed—a genuine sound Amelia was sure she hadn't heard since she was a high schooler. Amelia grinned.

"You're right, she would. You know I'd invite you, but I don't think that would go over too well."

Amelia shuddered as she pondered the life she'd been headed toward. Life as a mafioso's trophy wife. Rubbing her arms as if she were cold, she pictured her FBI self amid a sea of impeccably dressed Italian mobsters. Her path had been altered years ago. She recalled the look on Luca Passarelli's face as his words echoed through her head like a drumbeat in a cave.

"I don't ever want to see you in my city or near my son again. You got that, you little whore?"

Though she fought to keep the sudden distaste to herself, Alex's solemn expression told her she hadn't been successful.

"Sorry, I didn't mean to offend you. Really, if I thought I could, I'd send you a save-the-date. It sounds weird, but I think you and Liliana would get along great."

Amelia didn't want Alex to believe he was the source of her sudden mood change.

His father's lecherous threat had occurred almost twelve years ago, and she'd never bothered to sit down and explain the exchange to Alex.

Why? Did she think he wouldn't believe her?

Who cares if he doesn't? It's the truth, and now that he's getting married and has a foster daughter, he ought to know what a piece of shit his father is. Provided he doesn't have some idea already.

More than anything, revealing the truth to Alex would take a load of lingering guilt off Amelia's shoulders.

Another sigh slipped from her lips. "You didn't offend me. Picturing that just reminded me of something. Something I've been keeping to myself for a long time."

Alex's eyebrows knitted together. "What's that?"

"When I left and joined the military, I genuinely believed I was running for my life. Running from your father. Obviously, things have changed, and I came back to Chicago last year because I wasn't worried about Luca's threats anymore. I figured if he tried anything, I'd just arrest him and throw him in jail."

A muscle ticked in Alex's jaw. "He threatened you? Jesus Christ." He dragged a hand over his face. "Honestly, I wish I could say I was surprised. I've had a hell of a lot of time to ponder why you left. No offense."

Amelia snorted out a laugh. "None taken."

"It was one of the scenarios I pictured in my head. I asked Luca about it once, but he told me not to worry about it. Claimed you just took off because women were shifty by nature, or some line of BS like that. I didn't really buy it, but at the same time, I knew I wouldn't get anywhere with him. Talking to that man is like having a conversation with a piece of plywood."

"I can imagine." Amelia fought the urge to shift in her seat, suddenly ready for this conversation to be over. She was happy with the woman she'd become, even if her life's path had been shaped by the disgusting threats of a mafioso. She didn't want Alex to apologize, nor did she want him to express regret that their paths had separated when she was only eighteen.

"I would say I'm sorry, but I know I'm not the one who needs to apologize. And to be honest, it's incredibly unlikely you'll ever hear Luca say those words."

Not that Amelia wanted an apology from Alex's father either. She and Luca Passarelli would simply never cross paths again, if she had her way. "I appreciate it, really. But," she met Alex's gaze and shrugged, "it's in the past. As cheesy as it sounds, I'm looking ahead now, not behind me. And as luck would have it, ahead means tracking down an organ trafficker."

With a knowing smirk, Alex rose to his feet. "Right. Like I said, I'll keep my ears open. That's not the kind of shit the D'Amato family wants going on in their backyard, so if I catch a whiff of anything, I'll let you know."

"Thank you. I appreciate it." As Amelia stood, she extended her hand to Alex for a parting shake. They said their goodbyes, and Amelia shifted her focus fully away from her history with the D'Amato family.

She'd known before heading out to Adams Park that the

D'Amatos weren't involved with any form of organ trafficking, and she'd suspected the same for the Leóne family. The Leónes were despicable in their own right, but for all Amelia's time in the city, she'd never heard so much as a rumor of the Leónes dealing in organ trafficking.

Being the diligent agent she was, she'd needed to talk to Alex about it. Tick that box. Plus, now that she'd planted that bug in his ear, she had no doubt he'd let her know if he learned of anything moving forward.

Odds were, if there was a criminal organization kidnapping people and surgically removing all their organs to sell on the black market, Alex would've heard something. The fact that he was in the dark led her to believe they very well might be hunting for an individual.

It was a relief to know she was likely not dealing with the Russian mob or one of the Mexican drug cartels, but at the same time, the knowledge made the case even more perplexing.

Amelia would keep digging, even if she didn't like what her search uncovered.

There was no doubt in her mind that the person who'd murdered Kent Manning and the others would strike again.

Unless she stopped them first.

12

Grasping the metal banister as tightly as he could manage, Saul Avery slowly navigated the spiral staircase. His feet were unsteady, his weakened leg muscles straining under the weight of his body. He'd always been in shape, but at six-three, his broad-shouldered frame had never been light. And now, with his strength failing him, even just walking down the stairs was a Herculean feat.

Ironically, he'd bought this house because he'd been captivated by the grand staircase that led to an open-air loft on the second floor. Now that his health was deteriorating, he wished he'd bought a single-story ranch. His wife had insisted he move from their bedroom to the downstairs guest room or even have an elevator built, but Saul was stubborn. Taking all the medical supplies to the first floor was akin to admitting defeat, and installing an elevator to carry his sorry ass up and down one flight?

Bah.

Even though his fate was all but sealed, Saul had a history of stubbornness. It was part of what had made him so successful in his field.

By the time he reached the hardwood floor, perspiration had beaded on his brow, and his breathing was markedly more intense. His stomach churned as nausea threatened. Since when was going down the stairs supposed to be such an endeavor?

Gritting his teeth, Saul swallowed against the rising bile in the back of his throat.

Just make it to the damn breakfast bar, all right?

He already knew he'd find his wife in the kitchen—the scent of frying bacon had coaxed him out of bed. They had housekeepers, including a regular cook, but Mandy had taken over the humdrum chores, claiming they kept her busy while she was off work.

At the bottom of the stairs, Saul maintained his grip on the railing as he paused to collect himself. If he stumbled into the kitchen out of breath and beleaguered, his wife would immediately feel guilty for not helping him down the stairs. She'd reiterate her suggestion that they move his medical supplies to the guest room, and Saul would be awash with his own sense of remorse at making her worry so much.

God, how he wished their lives could just go back to normal.

Who'd have known he'd succumb to a heart attack at fifty-six? In Saul's mind, he'd still been young. Sure, he'd been a habitual smoker for almost forty years, but he didn't smoke that much. Hell, he'd even managed to kick the habit for a spell on three separate occasions. He didn't chain smoke, didn't smoke inside, didn't smoke in the car, and only went through half a pack a day.

Compared to the pack-a-day habit his old man had maintained until he'd died at seventy-two, Saul had figured he was ahead of the game. He still had time to quit the habit for good—he'd even picked up vaping, which cut back on cigarettes even more. In the days before the heart attack, he'd only been smoking a pack a week.

It didn't matter. Genetics had different plans for him.

With a weary sigh, Saul's eyes drooped closed, and he could almost smell the sterile hospital room again...

As his thoughts clawed their way toward consciousness, he used the persistent beep, beep, beep of a heart rate monitor to anchor himself in reality.

Though he couldn't recall the events leading up to being rushed to the emergency room, Saul knew right away he was in a hospital. He forced his eyes open, squinting at the muted daylight glowing behind the dark blue curtain on his left. The space was alien and familiar all at once, and he couldn't help but wonder if he was stuck in a dream that wouldn't end.

Maybe the intense pain in his chest hadn't been real. Maybe the shortness of breath and the crushing weight on his ribs had all been in his head.

Rubbing his forehead, Saul shoved aside the memory. His wife was waiting.

As he trudged toward the kitchen, the cardiologist's words echoed in his head...

"I'm sorry, Saul." Genuine sadness tugged at the edges of the middle-aged woman's brown eyes. She'd been the same doctor who'd looked after his mother during her final days, and her empathy had inspired Saul to make a sizable donation to the hospital.

He sat up a little straighter in his bed. "You don't have to sugar-coat it. I know it's bad." Even as panic threatened to wash over his thoughts like a tidal wave, he kept his expression as neutral as possible. With Mandy right beside him, her slender hand warm atop his, he couldn't show the depths of his fear.

The doctor tucked her pen into the pocket of her white lab coat. "All right. You suffered a significant cardiac event, and according to the results of our tests, the heart attack substantially weakened your heart. Unfortunately, due to a combination of factors, such as your history of smoking and genetic predisposition to heart disease, there's no procedure we can perform that will restore the function that was lost."

As Saul swallowed, his throat felt like it was coated in sandpaper. "What about a transplant?" He was no stranger to hospital procedures when it came to the organ transplant waiting list. Patients were prioritized based not only on their medical needs, but on how likely they were to make a good recovery, and how much their life would be extended with the transplant.

A fifty-six-year-old man wouldn't rank all that high on the list, even if he had donated generously to the hospital over the years.

The doctor glanced from Saul to Mandy and back, weariness plainly visible in the circles beneath her eyes. *"Unfortunately, Saul, based on your medical history and especially your previous treatment of bladder cancer, you won't be a viable candidate for the transplant list."*

That news, along with the time he had remaining, which was broken to him four weeks back, left him with a measly two-month life expectancy. Mandy had spoken to her boss, who'd offered his sympathies and granted her temporary leave.

Ever the enterprising woman, Mandy had used her time away from work to come up with a potential solution for Saul's failing health. And she found it.

The black market.

Her resourcefulness and resilience were two parts of her personality he'd fallen in love with, but Saul still hadn't reconciled the morality of his wife's suggestion. She'd proposed the idea three days ago, but Saul didn't exactly have the luxury of time on his side.

Tightening his hooded sweatshirt, Saul held back a sigh and shuffled toward the kitchen. His exhaustion from traversing the steps was nearly gone, and fortunately, the short trip to the kitchen wouldn't sap his energy.

From where she was facing the sink, his wife spun around at his arrival, a washcloth in one hand and a spatula in the other.

A smile graced Mandy's pretty face. "Good morning, sleepyhead." She gestured to the marble island in the center of the expansive kitchen. "I made some breakfast. Don't worry, it's turkey bacon. Then there's some toast and an egg white omelet with green peppers, onions, and some of the leftover fajita chicken from last night. I did a taste test, and it's delicious."

"Your cooking is always delicious, honey." After placing a light kiss on her cheek, Saul took a seat at the island.

True to his wife's word, the food was delicious. Though he tried to focus on the meal, he found it progressively more difficult to ignore the elephant in the room.

As Mandy finished wiping off the counter and oiling the cast-iron pan she'd used to cook, she turned her attention back to Saul. Her smile faded as her eyes met his, no doubt reading the gravity on his face.

"What's wrong?" She replaced the hand towel and made her way to the chair at his side.

That was a loaded question these days. "I think we should talk about the...idea you proposed a few days ago."

Now the seriousness in her eyes matched his. "You mean the transplant?" He opened his mouth to reply, but she held up a hand. "I've been doing a lot of research on it, and I've found some...options in the Chicago area. People who are experienced in this sort of thing, and who can help us."

"Experienced in what? Stealing people's organs?"

Mandy started shaking her head before he'd even finished. "No, no. Well...yes, but not living people. Listen, here's a statistic I found about organ donation. Ninety percent of people support organ donation, which is great, right?"

He nodded. "Right."

She lifted a finger. "Less than sixty percent of adults are actually registered as organ donors. Even if someone isn't registered, their family can still agree to donate if it's what they would've wanted. But the problem with that is approval can take time, and a human heart can only survive outside the body between four to six hours."

Saul followed his wife's logic. They were both registered as organ donors, but plenty of folks didn't bother or were morally opposed to the idea. "What does that mean for the black market? Are you saying the organ brokers on the black market are selling the organs of dead people who simply didn't check the donor box when they got their driver's licenses?"

"Exactly!" With a strained smile, Mandy squeezed his hand. "It's not cheap, and they make a hell of a lot of money on the sale. Probably more than they deserve, but still. If you think about it from a business standpoint, it's almost a fool-proof business model."

Again, she had a point. Selling organs was illegal in the United States, but if an organ broker was using their connections to sell the organs of a person who'd died unexpectedly, the legal consequences likely weren't nearly as dire as what they'd face for murder or kidnapping.

Those people were already dead. Why did they need to keep the heart in their chest when they were just going to be buried six feet under or cremated? They sure as hell weren't using it anymore.

Saul had plenty more questions, but he trusted his wife's judgment. She wouldn't intentionally put another person in harm's way. Hell, she didn't even eat pork because she felt bad for the way pigs were treated in slaughterhouses.

Still…was this the right decision?

"You're sure? This won't hurt anyone else?"

Mandy's eyes brightened. "I'm sure. I'll make certain of it."

Returning her smile, Saul allowed a thread of hope to wind its way through him. "All right. I trust you."

She'd never led him astray before, and Saul had to believe in her.

His life counted on it.

13

Kari hated the frictionless void where her brain had been suspended for the last…how long was it? How long had she been in this godforsaken room? She didn't have a clue. She could've been bound to this hospital bed for a day or an entire year. There was no way to mark the passing of time in this hell.

Consciousness came and went like a fickle dream, and even when she was awake, she floated on a cloud of nothingness. Her fight-or-flight response wouldn't kick in, and where she should've experienced a surge of adrenaline, the only thing surging at all was the monotone heart rate monitor beside her bed.

She focused on the sound, determined not to let it fade away. In her mind, she was a diver, and the *beep, beep, beep* was the glow of a searchlight piercing the water's surface. As long as she swam toward the light and didn't look back toward the darkness closing in on her, she could make it.

Pulling in a sharp breath, Kari's eyelids snapped open. The world around her was the same shade of dark gray it had been the first time she'd regained consciousness. In addition to the constant rhythmic beeping beside her bed, she could now make out the faint hum of machinery on the other side of the room.

Medical machinery. Remember? You're not alone in here.

But was the other person real, or had she imagined him?

At the memory of the unconscious, bandaged-up man she'd spotted the first time she'd awoken in this nightmare, Kari swallowed and turned her head in the direction of the mechanical whirring.

Her stomach dropped. The man was real, and he was hooked up to an entire collection of machines, presumably to keep him alive.

Kari recognized a dialysis machine, but the tubes sprouting from his neck and abdomen were less familiar. Each tube bore a deep red coloration and led to a device situated next to the dialysis machine. The more she studied the man, the harder it became for her to determine where the man ended, and the medical equipment began.

Why was the kidnapper going to such lengths to keep him alive?

And me?

The last and only time Kari recalled him making an appearance, he'd alluded to her life now having a greater purpose. Were the machines supposed to help realize that purpose?

What in the hell was going on here?

Near the foot of the man's bed, Kari spotted a portable stainless-steel table. She couldn't make out the items laid out atop it at first, but as she blinked away the film from her vision and squinted, she realized the items were surgical tools.

Hope combined with the greatest fear she'd ever known, causing her heart rate to pick up speed. She not only felt her pulse increase, but the *beep, beep, beep* of the machines gave her away.

Calm down. Slow your breathing and heart rate.

If he was here, she didn't want her kidnapper to know she was awake.

Once the beeping slowed down, she allowed herself to consider her options. She was shackled to this bed, but if she could get free, a weapon was only ten or so feet away. Turning her head just enough to see her wrists, she made note of the heavy-duty zip ties holding her in place.

Balling her hand into as tight a fist as she could, she tugged on the restraints that bound her left wrist. Her hopes sank. The bind offered only the slightest bit of slack.

Maybe if she tugged on it for a while…

Creak.

At the quiet disturbance of the door's hinges, Kari jerked her gaze away from her bound wrist. Though the newcomer was clad in scrubs and a mask, instead of the dress shirt and slacks he'd worn last time, Kari recognized him right away. He was the man from the park.

As his gaze drifted over to her, the corners of his eyes crinkled. He was smiling at her.

"Who…are…you?" Though she willed her words to come out with an air of authority, her tongue was thick and fuzzy, as if the roof of her mouth was coated in peanut butter.

"That's not for you to worry about, my dear. I'm glad to see you're awake, though. I always like to have an audience for the grand finale."

Grand finale? What the hell does that mean?

Kari couldn't find the strength to speak the words aloud. In fact, after struggling with the zip ties, she didn't have the energy for much of anything.

Not waiting for a response, the man wheeled the cart of surgical supplies over to the unconscious man's bedside.

Surely, he wasn't going to operate on that man right in front of her, was he? The space seemed clean enough, and he appeared to possess the proper equipment, but what kind of lunatic would perform surgery in this environment? And to what end? Didn't he need assistants?

Kari's head was spinning with all the questions she couldn't ask, and all the answers she was certain she'd never receive.

The man reached for an adjustable light above the bed. With his back to her, he switched on the UFO-shaped bulb, causing Kari's eyes to water from the sudden brightness. Then, after a soft click, opera music filled the room.

He's humming. Do something! He's not paying attention. This is your time to make a move.

But what exactly could she do?

Tears welled in Kari's eyes as she watched him move to a video camera and turn it on. He was recording. Who would watch such a thing?

Who will watch me? I'm going to die and he's humming along to the opera from Pretty Woman*. What the hell?*

Another feeble tug against the zip ties was a stark reminder of Kari's helplessness. She couldn't break free of the binds—not in her weakened state, and probably not even if she'd had all her strength. Given time, she might manage to wrench one of her wrists free, but he turned around before she could finish the thought.

"You know, the human body truly is a remarkable thing." After readjusting his mask and snapping on a fresh pair of gloves, he positioned the tray of surgical tools over the prone man, effectively covering his face from view. As he repositioned himself on the other side of the bed, so he was facing Kari, he didn't pay her the slightest bit of attention. "Human bodies are so resilient. Even in the most dire circumstances, they find a way to keep us alive. Take Irving here, as an example. Did you know that, right now, his lungs are gone?"

Kari's stomach did a somersault. That man had no lungs? How was he still alive?

With a low chuckle, the man reached for a scalpel. "The machine at his bedside is keeping him alive. It acts as both his heart and his lungs. It pulls blood from the body, oxygenates it, and then simulates the beat of his heart with the force it uses to push the blood back into the body. It's called extra-corporeal membrane oxygenation, or ECMO for short. In layman's terms, it's life support."

A sickening realization crept into Kari's mind. Right now, as she watched this lunatic slice into Irving's chest, she was staring down her own fate.

As the demonic surgeon brandished a set of forceps and began to peel Irving's skin back from the incision, revealing bright red muscle tissue glistening with blood, Kari could do little to pry her attention away from the macabre sight.

"This ECMO machine set me back a pretty penny. Using one of these things requires round-the-clock monitoring from trained personnel, but fortunately, I learned to operate it back during my residency."

So he *was* a doctor, not some uneducated psycho slicing into living people with no real idea what he was doing.

Not that the knowledge would help the man he was cutting into…or her.

Though Kari's logical mind told her she ought to parse through that information while she still had her wits about her, it was nearly impossible to focus on anything other than the unorthodox surgery being performed by the crazy son of a bitch who'd kidnapped her.

For the next God-only-knew how many minutes, Kari looked on, transfixed and terrified, as the surgeon reopened a previous incision, cutting away the tissue over

Irving's sternum. Once the white of the breastbone was visible, he snapped on a new pair of gloves and reached for a device that resembled a sterile version of a woodworking tool.

Only it wasn't a clamp for holding together two pieces of wood. Kari had seen plenty of medical dramas, and though the shows were far from accurate most of the time, she recognized a rib spreader when she saw one.

Mechanical cranking cut through the room's relative silence. Kari silently willed herself to close her eyes or look away, but she failed. Her fear became a living thing, a parasite slithering through her veins and rooting her in place.

Frozen in horror, she watched helplessly as the surgeon stuffed a sponge or gauze in the garish wound to stem its bleeding.

He switched back and forth between a litany of shiny silver tools as he continued his work inside Irving's chest. Seconds stretched into minutes, and somewhere along the line, Kari found the mental fortitude to turn her head. Though she wanted to close her eyes and let herself slip back into unconsciousness, the surge of terror, knowing what was occurring right beside her, kept her wide awake.

"Here we are. Have a look at this, my dear."

Bile threatened to climb up the back of Kari's throat. She considered obstinance—either by turning her head away or by squeezing her eyes shut—but how wise was a display of defiance when she was bound to a bed in a room with a man who'd just performed unassisted open-heart surgery on someone he'd likely kidnapped?

Swallowing the sudden bout of nausea, Kari reluctantly shifted her gaze from Irving's chest cavity to the madman's prized possession, which he was holding like an apple he was about to take a bite out of.

How she kept herself from vomiting at the scene in front

of her defied reason. Odds were, it had something to do with the sheer number of drugs in her system.

Vinyl gloves stained with crimson held the bloody mass of muscle tissue that was Irving's heart. The surgeon's mouth was still covered by his mask, but the maniacal gleam in his eyes was almost more disturbing than the fact that he held a human heart in his palms.

Another wave of nausea threatened Kari as the iron-tinged air penetrated her nostrils.

Unlike last time, she found the motivation to rip her gaze away within seconds. As she squeezed her eyes closed, tears slid down her cheeks. The surgeon was speaking, but over her thunderous pulse, Kari couldn't make out a word.

She didn't want to know what he was saying because chances were good it was more of the same insanity he'd been spouting since his arrival.

One sound broke through her resistance. The sound of a flatlining heart monitor. Irving's.

Balling her hands into fists, Kari kept her eyes shut and did her best to block out the world around her. Ironic, considering she'd just mused about how she wished she could maintain consciousness over all the sedatives she'd been dosed with so far.

Now all she wanted was to go back to sleep.

If he knocks you out again, you're never going to wake up.

The realization sent a jolt of panic through Kari like she'd just stuck her finger in a light socket. It was the most intense sensation she'd experienced since being drugged and brought to this place.

Hard plastic bit painfully into her skin as she pulled her wrist with all her might, attempting not to break the plastic, but to slide her hand out of the bind altogether. The sides of the bed groaned with her efforts, and for a beat, she believed she stood a chance.

"Uh-uh, none of that, my dear."

Irving was dead.

Just like you'll be if you stay here.

Jaw clenched so tightly she half expected to break a tooth, Kari gave one last monstrous pull on the ties. Though the rail on the side of the bed groaned again, all she accomplished was exacerbating the injury to her wrists.

She was so focused on using brute force to free herself, she hardly noticed the quiet footsteps as the lunatic surgeon approached her.

"Let me go!" Kari wanted to scream the words in his face, but the volume was barely above normal.

"You know I can't do that." Syringe in one hand, he loomed over her as he took hold of the IV tube.

"Look, you don't have to do this, all right? What do you want? Name it, and I'll get it. Just…just let me go, and I swear I won't tell anyone. I'll never say a word. I don't even know your name! Please, please…"

With a slight shake of his head, he plunged the needle into the medication slot of the IV. "It's too late for that. I have clients who are very eager for what you have to offer."

Kari started to protest, but before she could form the first word, the world around her swam, and the protestations died on her tongue.

14

In the two days since Amelia had spoken to Megan Manning, their case had made little headway. Cyber Crimes was scouring the dark web, and though they'd located a couple of promising leads, neither had panned out. Whoever was selling the victims' organs, they were dabbling in a part of the deep web that was incredibly difficult to reach.

Stretching out her legs, Amelia leaned back in her office chair to survey the murder board for the six-hundredth time. With her fellow agents out attending to their own tasks—everything from getting lunch to following up with Cyber Crimes—Amelia had the incident room to herself. She'd all but memorized every piece of information, and if someone asked her to recreate the image, she was confident she'd have no problem doing so.

"How in the hell are you guys connected? Are you even connected? There has to be something. Even an experienced organ trafficker has to find their victims somewhere."

But where?

"That's the million-dollar question." Amelia sighed. "The

five of you didn't know each other. I mean, trust me, after sifting through your social media posts from the last thousand years, we'd have found something, like if you guys were all part of a secret club. You're also not affiliated professionally. Pendleton was a mechanic. Then we've got Manning, who was a middle school gym teacher. Those two jobs couldn't be more unrelated if they tried."

Even the victims who'd lived geographically close to one another hadn't shared any common ground. They hadn't gone to the same grade school, junior high, high school, or college. They didn't even shop at the same damn grocery stores.

Charting the victims' routines was tedious work, and to Amelia's continued chagrin, it had yielded no groundbreaking leads.

Amelia narrowed her eyes at the whiteboard as if it had offended her. "All you have in common is that none of you had kids, and you were all around the same age. Kent Manning was married, Pendleton and Whitaker were divorced, and the others were single. You were all financially stable. None of you lived outside your means, and you were just…"

As the door at her back creaked open, Amelia left her observation unfinished. A whiff of garlic and onion heralded Zane and Sherry's arrival, each of them sporting bags full of takeout.

"Welcome back." Mouth suddenly watering, Amelia shoved aside a stack of case files to make room for their lunch.

Sherry tipped an invisible hat. "Why, thank you."

Before Amelia could ask what they'd ordered—since she'd never been to the Italian restaurant, Amelia had told Zane to surprise her—her gaze snapped to where her cell buzzed against the table. Glancing at Zane and Sherry, Amelia held up a finger as she reached for the device. The FBI-installed app revealed the caller's identity.

"Renee Stanley." She shot her friends a curious look. "That familiar to either of you?"

Zane's eyebrows drew together, but the contemplative expression lasted only a second before he snapped his fingers. "I saw her on Kent Manning's social media. She's a friend of his and Megan's."

Sudden excitement bubbled in Amelia's chest. Without waiting for Zane to elaborate, she swiped the screen and raised the phone to her ear. "This is Special Agent Storm."

A woman on the other line cleared her throat. "Hello, Agent Storm. I'm...um...sorry if I'm interrupting your lunch break or something."

It was lunchtime, but Amelia's food wasn't going anywhere. "No need to apologize. What can I help you with?" She tapped the speaker button so everyone could hear.

"Okay. Thank you." Her tone was notably more relaxed with the greeting out of the way. "I'm Renee Stanley. You probably know already, but I'm a friend of Megan and Kent Manning. I saw your card when I was visiting Megan yesterday evening, and when she wasn't paying attention, I took a picture of it."

Mentally, Amelia gave the woman props for her improvisation. "I'm glad you called."

"I'm sorry, I just feel...guilty about going behind her back, you know? Megan and I have been friends since we were in college together, and I became friends with Kent after they started dating. I really wanted to think the best of her because she's my friend, but she really weirded me out last night."

Amelia tried to ignore the sudden uptick in her pulse. "How so?"

"Well, like I said, I had taken a picture of your card. But it was weird because Megan was the one who brought it up. She pointed it out in her mail pile, which is usually where she keeps stuff like that. She wanted to know if anyone from the FBI had come to talk to me, and I told her no. That by itself wasn't weird, but…"

"But what? Did something happen?" Amelia kept her tone soothing. "Listen, Renee. The FBI is searching for the person who murdered Kent Manning. If you know anything that might help us, you need to tell me. The longer it takes us to catch this guy, the more likely it becomes that he'll hurt someone else."

The woman sniffled. "Y-you think he'll hurt more people?"

"I'm certain of it."

"Oh my god." After another sniffle, Renee cleared her throat. "Okay, okay. I'm sorry. This is just…hard. Kent and I were really good friends, and so were Megan and I, at least until last fall, or somewhere around there. That's when she started acting weird. Eventually, I asked her about it, and she told me she was having an affair."

"An affair? Do you know who with?"

"No, not really. But that's the thing that was so weird yesterday. She asked me if the cops…err, sorry, if the FBI had talked to me, and when I said no, she practically begged me not to tell you guys about the affair. She claimed the guy she was seeing wouldn't do anything to hurt Kent, so there was no point in turning his life upside down by making him the prime suspect. I just…thought that was really weird."

Weird and stupid.

Amelia pursed her lips, keeping the comment to herself. "Okay, if you don't know the man's name, do you know anything about him? Did Megan show you a picture, or did she talk about what he did for a living, where he might've gone to college? Anything?"

"She never said much about him because she could tell I didn't approve of her screwing someone else, even though Kent already knew." Although everyone in the room was hanging on Renee's every word, they collectively inhaled at this revelation. Unaware of the shock on Amelia's end of the call, Renee forged on. "Megan acted like it was a big secret, and honestly, I don't know why. I guess she was just trying to save face our friend group. But…she didn't say where he worked, but she did say he was some kind of doctor. A surgeon, I think."

Amelia was out of her chair, anticipation humming through her body. "That's very helpful. Any idea where he worked?"

"No. I'm sorry."

Amelia battered Renee with a host of additional questions in the hopes of jogging some piece of information loose. It didn't.

"Thank you, Renee. This is very helpful. If you can remember anything else, no matter how small, please give me a call."

"Okay. I will."

As Amelia killed the call, she realized Zane and Sherry had abandoned their lunches. Both their gazes were fixed on Amelia.

She stuffed her cell into the too-small pocket of her slacks. "We need to talk to Megan Manning again. She was having an affair with a surgeon."

"What's our theory, then?" Sherry gestured at the five names on the whiteboard. "These murders are all connected, there's no doubt about that. How would Megan's lover killing Kent fit into everything else?"

Zane drummed his fingers on the table. "If we're dealing with a criminal operation like a cartel, then they could have multiple people on their payroll to harvest organs. I know we've discussed that already, but it could possibly fit in this case too. If Megan's lover was in the organ-trafficking business before they even met, then he could've viewed it as a convenient way to get rid of Kent."

"True." Sherry snatched her handbag off the floor. "Well, Agent Storm, shall we go pay Megan Manning another visit?"

With the veritable feast on the table all but forgotten, Amelia shrugged on her jacket.

After all the tedium of the past couple of days, maybe they were about to find the missing link between their five victims.

15

As I closed out of the secure web browser, I opened the app on my laptop that monitored my patients. Between delivering Irving's heart to my contact at the transplant center and disposing of his body, I'd worked for nearly twenty-four hours straight.

Just as she had been when I left, Kari Hobill was sound asleep.

Her horrified reaction to the removal of Irving's heart had been expected. Like all the others, however, there was a morbid curiosity beneath the shock and disgust. Witnessing my patients experience that inexorable pull never ceased to amuse me.

Rubberneckers.

They could deny it all they wanted, but they were no better than the men and women locked away for cold-blooded murder.

I chuckled quietly to myself. Better to embrace the demon that lurked within our psyches than feign morality. They could hate me all they wanted, but at least I was honest with myself.

Right after removing Irving's heart, I'd sealed the wound with gauze and plastic wrap to keep the mess to a minimum. Thanks to that little trick, I didn't have to worry about any blood seeping from the tarp I used to transport him. Such a mishap didn't seem like a catastrophe, but I didn't want to waste my time cleaning upholstery when I could devote the same effort to far more valuable activities.

"Well, my dear Kari, it won't be long until someone is on the sideline watching your heart as it's cut from your chest."

As I'd anticipated, the demand for Kari's heart and lungs was far higher than usual. The size of her kidneys wasn't as impactful, so I'd decided to go ahead with selling them both before I started to close out the bids on her more valuable assets.

I'd be keeping her alive for a bit longer than usual, but the extra effort would pay off in spades.

Back when I'd started my little side business, I'd been surprised to learn of the prevalence of the black-market organ trade. But because of the secretive nature of the industry, exact numbers were difficult for the authorities to establish. In fact, there were those who still considered the entire industry a myth.

Based on the research I'd done, as well as what I'd learned from my Russian friend, Bogdan, most organ brokers procured their merchandise from migrants or those who'd been trafficked.

When I'd discovered this snippet of information, I'd wrinkled my nose in disgust.

I wasn't like those *traffickers*. My medical experience was hard-earned and robust, and my business held a scientific purpose. A purpose those mafiosos would never understand.

They weren't medical doctors. I was.

Though my day job had me dealing with simpletons in search of cosmetic surgery, I realized the importance of finding a healthy donor for a prospective organ transplant. I was still a surgeon, and I took pride in my work. Could those mafioso hacks say the same?

"I'm sure there are some surgeons out there who'd be willing to sell their skills for an extra profit." I glanced at the potted cactus and let out a derisive snort. "But that's all they care about. Profit. They don't realize how much they could learn, or how much they could impact the scientific community, if they just applied themselves."

My gaze drifted back to the camera feed on my laptop, where Kari Hobill's unconscious form rested beneath a pastel-blue blanket.

A smile tugged at my lips. "But we know, don't we, my dear? We know how valuable your experience will be, even long after you're gone. Just imagine everything future generations will be able to glean from our time together. When we better understand the limits of human endurance, we'll be better suited to hone our methods of keeping the sick alive while we treat them. The cartels don't understand that. The cops don't understand it either."

Thinking of the cartels dragged a sigh out of my throat.

Bogdan had warned me to tread carefully when I'd expressed my interest in expanding my work. He'd claimed the Russian mob had a stake in the worldwide organ trade, but he couldn't be sure if the Bratvas were actively involved in the industry in my area. According to him, the last thing I wanted to do was step on the Russian mob's toes.

Goose bumps prickled my forearms, but not from fear—from exuberance. The future held great things for Bogdan and me.

Perhaps I was being willfully ignorant, but the Russians didn't frighten me. In my eyes, they were more of a nuisance than anything.

I returned my attention to the unconscious Kari, and I let

myself imagine a sprawling room filled with patients just like her. People whose lungs and kidneys were gone, but whose brains still pulsed with activity.

How much could I take away while still maintaining some level of consciousness?

Just the question alone sent a shot of childlike delight through me.

"You look lonely, my dear. I think it's high time I found you a new companion, now that Irving is gone. Don't worry. I have several candidates in mind."

I stretched both arms above my head until my lower back popped. My time with dear Kari would be nearing an end soon, but I had the means to acquire another patient well before her expiration date.

Opening another special app from my secure folder, I watched as a map populated with a dozen or so tiny dots. It'd been so easy, really. Send a text message, and with just a tap of their finger, I had access to their location.

And when Bogdan got to America, I'd have access to even more resources. His idea to film the surgical procedures I performed and charge a dark web audience to watch was just short of brilliant. The thought had crossed my mind in the past, but I wasn't quite as knowledgeable about the snuff film industry as my Russian friend.

Once Bogdan was here, the sky would be the limit.

In the meantime, which of these little dots would be my next patient?

16

With Sherry Cowen on her heels, Amelia pushed open the door to the interview room. The trip to speak with Megan Manning had been mostly uneventful. When Amelia and Sherry had sternly advised Megan that they'd be conducting this interview at the FBI office, Megan had offered only a weak protest.

Either the woman knew she'd been caught in a lie, or she was some sort of criminal mastermind who remained dedicated to her fictitious role no matter the scrutiny leveled at her.

On the drive to the Manning residence, Amelia had proposed the idea to Sherry. Based on Dr. Francis's reports of the victims so far, they could safely say a great deal of work had gone into the organ removal. Could so much effort be indicative of two perpetrators instead of one? Clearly, Megan didn't have the skill set to perform surgery on another human being, but who knew if she'd been trained to assist someone who did possess the necessary skill? Like her alleged surgeon boyfriend...

As Amelia stepped into the mostly bare interview room,

anticipation hummed beneath her skin. Megan didn't meet the profile of their killer at first blush, but there was always more to a case than what was visible on the surface. Especially a case as complicated as this.

Megan Manning's wide brown eyes snapped away from where they'd been fixed on the two-way mirror. Twisting the gold band around her left ring finger, the woman glanced from Sherry to Amelia, but she didn't speak.

The obvious nervousness in Megan's tense posture quickly cast a shadow of doubt on Amelia's theory that the woman was a secret criminal genius.

Even if she isn't an evil mastermind, she's got some explaining to do.

Amelia pulled out a chair across from Megan. "Sorry to keep you waiting. Can we get you anything to drink? Water, coffee, pop?" The offer wasn't so much to be accommodating as it was a clever method to collect DNA evidence. No DNA had been found on the victims so far, but Amelia preferred to be prepared for anything.

Megan clasped her hands together. "No, thank you."

Dropping a legal notepad onto the table, Sherry took her seat. "Before we get started, I'm going to read you your rights. It's standard protocol so that, once we find your husband's killer, their defense attorney can't say we didn't treat everyone within the investigation equally. That could create reasonable doubt for the jury, and we don't want that to happen."

That was only half true. The bigger purpose of getting this part of the procedure completed was so that they could use anything Megan said during the interview in court, if it came to that.

"But I'm not under arrest, am I?"

Amelia forced a warm smile. "Of course not. Like Sherry said, this is standard practice."

Megan still looked shaken as Sherry went through the official reading of her rights. When Megan signed the document stating she'd been informed about them and about the interview being recorded, Amelia relaxed back into her chair.

"All right, we'll get started, then. Do you know why you're here today, Megan?"

The woman's gulp was practically audible, reminding Amelia of the cartoons she used to watch with her brother. "So you can ask me some questions about my husband."

If Amelia was completely confident she was dealing with a hardened criminal, she might've offered up a sarcastic response. Still unsure what to make of Megan, she would be much gentler...at first.

To get under Megan's skin without her shutting them out completely, Amelia had to walk a fine line between intimidating and understanding. In opposition to what most television shows depicted, an interrogation was more of a seduction than a clash of wills.

"That's right." Amelia kept her voice as gentle as if she were speaking to a best friend. "We spoke with you three days ago, but we've since come across new information that makes us worry that you weren't entirely forthcoming during that interview. I know how stressful this has all been for you, so we wanted to give you another chance to be straight with us."

The color drained from Megan's knuckles, her shoulders stiffening. "What do you mean? I told you why I was visiting my sister when Kent was missing, and..." Her eyebrows creased, sudden understanding in her expression. "You don't...you can't think I had anything to do with Kent being murdered, can you? I wasn't even in the state when he was killed."

As unshed tears sprang to Megan's eyes, Amelia leaned

forward, her expression soft. "Your alibi has been verified. We know you were out of town when Kent died, but that doesn't mean you've been truthful about everything. I'm going to ask you a difficult question, and I'm only going to ask it once. We already know the answer, so we're giving you the opportunity to be honest."

Megan swiped beneath her eyes and sniffled. If the woman was faking her anxiety, the performance was worthy of an Oscar. "Okay. What's the question?"

Folding her hands, Amelia met Megan's gaze and held it. "Are you having an affair?"

Blond hair fell over Megan's face as she hung her head. "Yes." Between her small voice and slumped posture, Megan embodied the definition of defeated.

The sense of shame took Amelia by surprise, though she made sure not to let the sentiment show. "Is there a reason you neglected to mention this when we came to speak before?"

As she worried her teeth over her bottom lip, Megan kept her gaze fixed on her hands. "I know he didn't have anything to do with...with Kent. He's not like that. He's a good person, and he'd never hurt anyone, especially not Kent."

Amelia tempered a sudden spark of annoyance. "To be frank, that's not your judgment call to make."

Before Amelia could continue, Megan's eyes snapped up to shift back and forth between the two agents. "No, he wouldn't. Look, I've seen enough true crime documentaries and cop shows. I know the first place the cops look is the spouse, and if that spouse is having an affair..." She brushed away another round of tears, and Amelia didn't miss the tremor in her hand. "I knew if I said anything about him, he'd be your number one suspect."

"And if he's responsible for killing Kent, then your omission could cost the life of another innocent person." This time, Amelia didn't bother to keep the sharpness out of her tone. If Megan's lover was an organ trafficker, then Amelia's statement was accurate. She'd strike the fear of God into Megan Manning if that was what it took to get the woman to come clean.

"He wouldn't, he didn't do—"

"He matches our profile of the killer," Sherry said. "And you withheld your relationship with him. We're going to find out who he is, one way or another, so I highly suggest you cooperate this time around."

With a sniffle, Megan nodded. "All right. What do you want to know?"

As Sherry's pen clicked, Amelia took her cue. "Start with his name."

"Tim Moreno."

"And what does Tim Moreno do for a living?"

Megan wrung her hands, and for a beat, Amelia wondered if she was about to clam up. After a tense moment of silence, Megan finally met Amelia's gaze. "He's a plastic surgeon. He works at a private clinic here in Chicago called Skin Deep."

As Sherry scrawled in her notepad, Amelia studied Megan closely. Most of the nervous tension from the start of the interview had given way to weariness, and if Amelia had to guess, the woman had completely let down her guard.

I doubt a woman guilty of aiding her lover in kidnapping and murder would come across as quite this vulnerable.

Not that Amelia was ready to completely dismiss the possibility. Stranger things had happened.

"How long have you two been seeing one another, and how did you meet?"

Megan sighed, dropping her face into her hands. "His daughter goes to the school where Kent teaches, and she was in Kent's gym class last year. I was helping Kent chaperone at one of the school dances last October, and Tim was chaperoning too. Kent was busy talking to everyone, he was just one of those people, and I'd just stand there. Anyway, I went to get some air, and Tim was outside too. We exchanged numbers, and..." She shrugged weakly. "One thing led to another, I guess."

"I understand." Amelia figured the start of the relationship was innocuous enough, but even the most sinister relationships had benign beginnings. "Is there a reason you remained married to Kent during this affair? I recall from our first interaction that you were adamant you'd file for divorce if your marriage wasn't working out."

Megan pushed the strands of hair from her face. "I know. But...it was more complicated than that. Tim is...in a difficult marriage, and he has a daughter. It wasn't as easy for him as it would've been for me. He'd have had to pay alimony, and there'd be the custody battle. I guess we were just sort of stuck where we were. He couldn't leave his wife, so I wasn't going to leave Kent either."

Sherry tapped her pen against the notepad, drawing Megan's attention to her. "Did Kent know about the affair?"

"Yes." The word was barely above a whisper, and for the second time, Megan hung her head in shame. "He found out a few months ago. We went to marriage counseling at first, and I swear I tried. I swear. But...I don't think Kent could get past the affair. A few weeks ago, he told me he didn't want to be married to me anymore."

"I see." So far, Amelia was having a difficult time pinpointing a motive for Tim Moreno. If Tim would've wanted anyone dead, Amelia assumed it would be his wife so he could eliminate the financial threat posed by a divorce. Why Moreno would target Kent was beyond her understanding. "We didn't find any record of divorce proceedings when we ran a background check on you and Kent. Is there a reason for that? Did Kent have second thoughts?"

Megan heaved a sigh. "No, he didn't. But he wanted to make sure I'd be okay financially. We were talking things through, just trying to break down how we'd split everything."

It sure didn't seem like Megan's lover had a reason to resort to murdering Kent Manning, but Amelia'd come across her fair share of bizarre motives during her tenure with the FBI. Besides, if Tim Moreno truly was a trafficker who abducted and killed innocent people to sell their organs, then there was no telling what could set him off.

Amelia and Sherry ran through the rest of their questions, but by the time they released Megan and stepped back into the hall, Amelia was no more convinced of Tim and Megan's involvement than she'd been beforehand. If anything, she was less certain Megan had been involved in Kent's murder.

Can't say the same for Tim Moreno.

After making their way to the incident room mostly in silence, Amelia and Sherry gave the rest of the team—Dean, Zane, and Layton—a rundown of their little chat with Megan.

Agent Layton's chair squeaked as he leaned back, observing the whiteboard. "Well, from what we can see so far, Tim Moreno does fit the profile. He lives in the southern part of Chicago, which would also line up with all the bodies being dumped south of the city. He's been a plastic surgeon for seventeen years, according to the clinic's website. Though he mainly works on a person's surface, he would have been trained in general surgery as well."

On the other side of the table, Zane tapped a few keys on his laptop. "I'm still digging, but at a glance, it sure looks like

Moreno must be raking in the cash if he's able to afford the type of lifestyle he and his family are living."

Amelia craned her neck to see his screen. "What do you mean?"

"Well, for starters, his wife, Julia, is a stay-at-home mom, and as of this school year, their daughter is attending a prestigious private school. The tuition, plus the mortgage on their house, plus all those vacation pictures Dean noticed on Julia's social media accounts, plus the late model Mercedes and Audi they both drive…" Zane shot them a knowing look.

"That's got to be expensive." Amelia had lived in Chicago all her life, and she was pointedly aware of how pricy living in the city could become. "But he's a plastic surgeon for a private clinic, so he makes good money, right?"

Dean tapped at his screen. "The average salary for a Chicago plastic surgeon is four-fifty. He's got to have a side gig or some sort of investment. Maybe property rentals or something along those lines. Whatever it is, he didn't report it on his taxes this year."

Amelia considered all the options. "Maybe an inheritance. We need his financials."

Sherry held up a finger. "I'll get started on that now. It's possible he just neglected to include it when he filed his taxes, and it wouldn't be the first time. I'll see if I can find some legal form of revenue to explain the discrepancy."

With renewed determination, Amelia opened her laptop. "I'll help you dig into Moreno's background."

Pushing himself away from the table, Zane smiled at Dean. "I guess that leaves us to go pick up the lover boy and bring him in for a little chat."

Provided he doesn't know we picked up Megan earlier. If he thinks the FBI is onto him, he might've disappeared already.

Amelia kept the pessimism to herself as Zane and Dean took their leave. At first blush, Tim Moreno was a solid match to the perpetrator they sought, but Amelia wondered if this was too easy. Was there a missing puzzle piece they hadn't noticed?

If Moreno truly was an organ trafficker, why would he suddenly risk his livelihood to eliminate Kent Manning? Had Kent threatened to tell Tim's wife about the affair? The relationship was out in the open between Megan and Kent, but Moreno was likely still keeping the secret from his own spouse. Still, having an affair, a full-time job, being a husband and father, and running a thriving organ-trafficking business on the side—it didn't seem like there'd be enough hours in his day for all that.

But where there's a will there's a way.

Had Megan Manning's desire to sleep with Tim Moreno unwittingly put her estranged husband in the crosshairs of a mass murderer?

There was only one way to get to the bottom of Amelia's questions.

They needed answers from Tim Moreno.

———

17

L eaning against the beige drywall of the interview room, Zane spared a glance at the two-way mirror behind which Layton Redker sat. The screech of metal on tile jerked his attention back to the small table as Dean Steelman took a seat across from the newest person of interest in their case, Tim Moreno.

When Moreno had greeted them at the front door of his lavish residence, Zane had been taken aback. Between Moreno's driver's license photo and the images Zane had seen on Julia Suarez-Moreno's social media, Zane had expected someone whose appearance was quite different. The pudgy, balding man seated across from Dean was far from the pictures Zane had pored over when researching the plastic surgeon. Sometimes, Zane forgot how many aspects of a person's appearance could be hidden by clever camera angles, filters, and a simple hat.

When Zane cleared his throat, Moreno's nervous gaze shifted over to him. A slight sheen of sweat had formed on the man's forehead since they'd entered the interview room, and his right foot had barely stopped moving since he'd taken his seat.

A person capable of abducting and slicing apart another human being should've commanded nerves of steel, but Moreno was more like a tub of butter beneath a heat lamp.

"Mr. Moreno, do you know why you're here with us this afternoon?" Dean's steady baritone cut through the silence.

"That's Dr. Moreno." Licking his lips, Moreno returned his focus to Dean and shook his head. "No. You didn't tell me. You just told me I could come with you, or you'd send a squad car to pick me up 'in style.' I think those were your exact words, weren't they?"

Zane held back a chuckle. So the suspiciously wealthy surgeon was a smartass.

"Those were my exact words, yes. I'm glad you were paying attention." Dean's expression remained neutral as he spoke.

Moreno blinked a few times, confusion evident in his demeanor, but he didn't respond. Apparently, he hadn't expected one of the Feds to meet his sarcasm.

Dean didn't give the man a moment to put his thoughts together. "What's your relationship with Megan Manning?"

Start small. See if he lies about the little things. Smart.

"My relationship with who?" Moreno's foot had paused but went right back to *tap-tap-tapping* as he folded his hands and attempted nonchalance.

For the second time, Zane barely suppressed a laugh. "Really, mister...um, Dr. Moreno? You're going to play dumb with us about something this small? You know that's not a good look, and you ought to know damn well we didn't haul you into the FBI office to talk about how we think the Cubbies are going to do this season." He rubbed his hands together, as if he was about to begin a laborious task. "One

more time, all right? What is...your relationship...with...
Megan...Manning?"

Indignation flickered behind Moreno's dark eyes as his
hands balled into fists. "Oh, Megan Manning. I must've heard
you wrong."

Dean's smile was all teeth. "Guess it's that Southern *twang*,
ain't it?" He gestured to Zane. "You heard my partner. Megan
Manning. Tell us what we don't already know."

A muscle ticked in Moreno's jaw. "It's not much of a relationship. My daughter used to attend the public school
where Megan's husband worked. I met her when I was chaperoning at one of the middle school dances."

Silence descended on them, and Zane wondered if they
were going to be forced to pry the information out of the
plastic surgeon like a dentist performing a tooth extraction.

Zane crossed his arms. "And? Look, we're not the infi-
delity police. If you're being obstinate about the little things,
like how you've been sleeping with Megan Manning for the
last year, what do you think that tells us?"

He could swear the grinding of Moreno's teeth was audible. The man peered at the two-way mirror, then at Dean. "Is
my wife on the other side of that glass? Is she going to hear
any of this?"

*Why in God's name would we let your wife listen in on an
interrogation?*

Zane swallowed the retort. "No. Your wife isn't going to
hear this. Now, like my partner said, spit it out."

As Moreno ran a hand through his thinning hair, he let
out a shaky sigh. "All right. I've been...seeing Megan for, um,
I don't know, since the fall. Like I said, we met at one of my
daughter's school dances. My wife and I have been having
marital issues for a long time, and Megan was just so...
refreshing. I've been trying to break it off, but, well...you
understand, right?"

Zane didn't dignify that with a response. "What about her husband, Kent Manning? How well did you know him?"

Posture tensing, Moreno shrugged. "I didn't."

Whether the man was lying, or the subject of his lover's dead husband simply made him nervous, Zane couldn't quite tell. "Never met him? Not even in passing?"

"Not even in passing."

Dean propped his elbows on the table. "You know Kent Manning was murdered, right? You seem like a smart fella, so I'm sure you know that when someone turns up murdered, the first person we look into is the spouse. And if that spouse is having an affair...well."

Moreno's Adam's apple bobbed as he swallowed. "You can't possibly think I had anything to do with what happened to that poor man. I might've been having an affair with his wife, but I had no reason to wish ill on him. I swear, I've never even met the guy!"

The man's apprehension had just gone from a five out of ten to an eleven, but Zane had come to realize such a change was normal when the word *murder* surfaced.

"Where were you on March twenty-fourth?"

Moreno sputtered. "I have no idea."

"I need you to find out."

Before Zane could ask for alibis about the other victims, Moreno practically shouted, "Look, I've told you the truth so far, okay?" He flattened his palms against the table. "But if you want to ask me any more questions, I'd like to have my lawyer present."

Though Zane wasn't the type of criminal investigator to automatically assume everyone who requested a lawyer was hiding something—the right to legal counsel existed for a reason—Tim Moreno radiated so much nervous energy, Zane could practically taste it. And he could definitely smell it.

His gut insisted Moreno was keeping a secret from them, and as he recalled the details of Moreno's posh lifestyle, he was determined to find out what the man was hiding.

Zane slid his phone across the table and waited while the doctor called his lawyer. Once the call ended, he collected his phone and rose from his chair.

Rapping his knuckles against the table, Dean pushed to his feet as well. "All right. I guess we'll pick this back up when your attorney gets here."

With a sideways glance at Moreno, Zane followed Dean out into the hall. As soon as the door latched closed, Dean shook his index finger at the interview room. "That asshole's hiding something."

"Agreed." Zane strode a few steps to another door, knocking before he let himself into the dim observation room.

Layton straightened in his chair, white light from the screen of his laptop catching the lenses of his glasses as he turned to Zane and Dean. "That sure was interesting."

Zane wasted no time before he snatched up his paper cup of coffee and took a long drink. The beverage was lukewarm, but he didn't mind. "Indeed." He tilted his chin at the two-way glass. "Find anything else on Dr. Moreno while we were chatting with him?"

"A little, but it's mostly just info to confirm what we already suspected." Layton tapped his wrist. "You saw that watch he's wearing, right? Well, I found one of Julia Suarez-Moreno's Instagram posts where she gave him that for his birthday a few months ago. MSRP for that thing is right around twenty grand."

Resisting the urge to glance at his own pricey watch, Zane took another swig of coffee. With a mother who was a successful, retired hedge fund manager, speculating on the spending habits of the exceptionally wealthy was firmly in

Zane's wheelhouse. "What kind of salary is he reporting to the IRS?"

"A little less than three hundred grand per year. Mortgage on his house is twelve thousand per month, plus property taxes, utilities, and other expenses. Then there's his and his wife's cars, which set them back a couple grand every month after insurance. His wife totaled a car about two years ago, and she was at fault for the accident, so their insurance payments are sky-high."

Dean let out a low whistle. "No way in hell he's going on all these vacations, sending his kid to a private school, and managing to pay for all that shit when he's making less than five hundred K annually. I could see it if he was single and living by himself, maybe, but not with a wife and kid."

"Right." Layton rubbed his chin, appearing thoughtful. "On paper, Tim Moreno is a fit for the profile I put together on the killer. But watching his demeanor during the interview, it's...curious. If he's the unsub we're looking for, then I think he almost definitely works for someone else. He doesn't seem to have the constitution for operating an organ-trafficking business from the ground up."

"I was under the same impression." Zane studied Moreno through the two-way mirror, noting the man's foot was still tapping out its rapid cadence. "I've been working Organized Crime for quite a while, and I can tell you I've never met a gangster who wilts under pressure quite like Dr. Moreno in there."

Not that the observation was reassuring. If Tim Moreno was nervous in the presence of the FBI, then Zane could only imagine what he was like when he had to deal with a mob boss. Odds were, if he was working for a criminal organization, he'd be too frightened to give up any information about his employer, especially once his lawyer was in the room.

During the wait for Moreno's attorney, Zane and his two

companions broke down the remainder of the surgeon's finances, confirming a significant discrepancy for the most recent fiscal year. Strangely enough, in years prior, the Moreno family's budget was consistent with Tim's salary.

So what had changed?

As a lanky man in an expensive suit arrived and took a seat next to Moreno, Zane was ready to find out. Unfortunately, they'd have to wait until the doctor and attorney had conferred first.

"Let's get out of here so the lawyer can't accuse us of violating attorney-client privilege." Zane headed straight to the coffeepot. He was going to need all the caffeine he could get.

Half an hour later, Moreno was ready. Armed with a few printouts of the surgeon's recent expenses, Zane followed Dean into the interview room.

Easing the door closed, Zane flashed Moreno and his lawyer a disarming smile. "Nice to see you again, Dr. Moreno." He gestured to the lawyer. "And you must be his counsel."

"I am. Nathanial Holloway, senior defense counsel at McLean and Associates."

"Right. I'm Special Agent Palmer, and this is my partner, Special Agent Steelman. Before you got here, we were discussing Kent Manning with your client. I was hoping we could pick up right where we left off." Zane handed the attorney a sheet of paper. "And we need to know where your client was on these specific dates."

Holloway examined the dates. "Why so many?"

"We have several victims who died in the same manner as Mr. Manning. We just need to check off every box."

Moreno's mouth popped open while the lawyer's stony expression grew stonier. Holloway held up a hand to keep his client from speaking. "If that's what you want, I'm sure it won't be a problem. My client doesn't know anything about Kent Manning, and he certainly wasn't involved in Mr. Manning's, or anyone else's, murder."

Dean pulled out a chair but didn't sit. "All right, sure. Change of subject for a second, then." He held up the papers. "While we were waiting for you, we had a chance to take a look through Mr. Moreno's finances." He handed the lawyer a copy of the warrant before he could ask.

All the color drained from Tim Moreno's cheeks, and his foot ceased its rhythm against the tiled floor.

Finances had hit a nerve, and as far as Zane was concerned, the reaction was even more intense than Moreno's paranoia when Kent Manning had been mentioned.

Interesting.

Dropping down to sit, Dean leafed through the papers as he explained Layton's findings to Moreno and his lawyer. Upon listing each expense, Moreno shrank a little more. He reminded Zane of a balloon left over from a party.

As Dean neared the end of his diatribe, Zane took his spot across from Moreno.

"So," Dean tapped the sheet of paper, "do you mind telling us how your client has been managing to juggle all these expenses?"

Holloway sighed as if the entire situation bored him. "Well, Agents, there are these things called credit cards, and—"

Zane snapped his fingers. "No, we're not doing that. We already checked. Your client has zero credit card debt. In fact, his only debt is what he owes on his house and his two vehicles. And he hasn't been late on a payment yet."

Holloway scoffed, annoyance plain on his face. "Fine. Investments, then. Rental properties. My client is a successful plastic surgeon who works for an equally successful clinic. It would be asinine to think he hadn't invested some of those funds over the years."

"Funny you should mention that." Zane ignored Holloway and flashed Moreno a grin. "Investment happens to be my family's specialty. We didn't have to dig very deep to find that your client hasn't made any investments. In fact, Dr. Moreno recently left his position as a partner at a different cosmetic surgery clinic, Plastic Surgery Institute of Chicago. He'd been working there for quite a while, and from what we've gathered so far, he took a hefty pay cut. Strange that his increased spending started after the change."

"Is there a point to this? I was led to believe my client had been brought in to discuss Kent Manning's tragic death, not his personal finances."

"As luck would have it, those two things are related." Zane leaned forward, pinning Moreno with a hard stare. "We have reason to believe that Kent Manning's death was related to a handful of others. Without going into too much detail, I can tell you that the person who killed them has done so for a profit. Based on the manner in which the bodies were disposed, as well as the substances found in their tox screens, the killer possessed substantial medical knowledge and capability."

Moreno's eyes popped open so wide that Zane was surprised they didn't roll right out of his head. "W-what? Is that...no, no, you've got the wrong guy."

Holloway silenced his client with an upraised hand. "Don't worry, Tim. You don't need to reply to that."

"I want them to know I didn't kill anybody! I've made some mistakes and I'm not perfect, I'll admit it. I've been having an affair, and I've done some things I'm not proud of, but I sure as hell didn't kill anyone!" Moreno's sudden outburst was underscored by so much desperation, Zane almost believed him.

Without lowering his hand, Holloway shot his client a stern glare. "I know, but you need to let me handle this."

Slumping down in his chair, Moreno muttered an apology, and Holloway returned his attention to Zane and Dean.

"Listen, Agents. The reason my client left his position at the Plastic Surgery Institute of Chicago is…complicated. Suffice it to say, he and the owner had a disagreement. Someone at the clinic was embezzling funds, and the owner was dead set on my client being the guilty party. As I'm sure you've noticed, no charges were ever filed against my client because the owner couldn't prove his outlandish claims. Upon leaving the clinic, my client was awarded a severance package which should explain the discrepancies you've seen in your research thus far."

Embezzlement? Was that why Moreno had been so jumpy when his finances were mentioned?

Zane didn't buy the severance explanation for a second, but Moreno stealing money from his old employer made sense.

Moreno motioned for his attorney to come closer, and the two began a whispered conversation that Zane strained to hear. A few minutes later, the attorney straightened. "My client would like to share a *hypothetical* scenario of how someone might skim profits."

Zane shrugged. "That's fine." He didn't give a true shit about the man's finances. He just needed him to talk.

"In scenarios like this," Moreno wiped the sweat from his forehead with his sleeve, "a person would likely hide the funds from their wife and not spend any of the money. They would hope this would allow them to avoid suspicion. Once the former employer confronted them, the person would plead ignorance. Without proof, the employer would agree to a separation of employment without charges. Then, hypothetically, the person would use the separation agreement as the explanation to the spouse about the influx of cash. Once the person was cleared of suspicion, the floodgates would open, and the two could begin freely spending the ill-gotten gains."

As Zane listened to the hypothetical confession, he knew they didn't have enough evidence to hold Tim Moreno beyond the interview. In fact, Zane's instincts cast doubt on Moreno's involvement in any of the murders. Based on the evidence collected from each victim so far, all five homicides were undoubtedly linked to the same killer.

If Moreno hadn't killed the others, then it was unlikely he'd killed Kent. Not to mention the man's demeanor. Just because Moreno could keep calm in an operating room didn't mean he was cut out for murder.

Before the interview had even finished, Zane had the sinking suspicion they'd come upon a dead end. Locating the individual who'd murdered and cut apart five innocent people so early in the investigation would be too convenient. Whoever the perpetrator was, they'd been fine-tuning their skills for a while.

Unless Zane and the team located a valid lead soon, the killer would continue to hone their craft, and more innocent people would die.

18

As she blew on the steaming mug in her hands, Amelia gazed at the whiteboard. After digging deeper into the backgrounds of the five victims, she and the others hadn't been able to establish a link between any of them and Tim Moreno or Megan Manning.

Cyber Crimes was scouring the dark web for organ-trafficking activity around the Chicago area, but according to the brief they'd been given the night before, there were still spaces online where a person with the right knowledge could hide.

In the meantime, it was up to Amelia and the rest of the team to chase down every potential lead they could find, starting with visiting the location where Kent Manning had last been seen. They'd do the same for the other victims, but they wanted to start with the latest disappearance. Amelia figured if any evidence existed, it would likely be from the most recent victim.

Though the Chicago Police Department had done a cursory investigation when Kent was reported missing, the case notes were sparse.

The door at Amelia's back creaked as it opened, and she turned as Dean stepped into the room.

Glancing at the empty table, Dean lifted an eyebrow. "They're still not back yet?"

Amelia shrugged and sipped her coffee, grateful for the warmth on the chilly spring morning. "I guess not. To be fair, it *is* nine in the morning, and there's probably a line at the donut shop this time of day."

Dean rubbed his chin. "True. I don't suppose you had an epiphany while I was out stretching my legs?"

"Unfortunately, no." Amelia lifted a finger from the warm mug. "But we might be able to learn something by talking to the people who were working at the high school on the night Kent Manning went missing. He used the high school gym to work out in, since it has better equipment than the gym at the junior high, and that's the last place Megan Manning recalled him going before he vanished."

Appearing thoughtful, Dean strode over to where Kent's information was scrawled on the whiteboard. "We haven't been able to link the other vics to Tim Moreno, and he's got an alibi for the night Kent went missing. He's also accounted for around Manning's time of death. Sherry talked to his wife last night, and it sounds like she didn't know anything about the affair. Not that she'd be a suspect anyway, considering her undergrad is in art history. It's a far cry from an MD."

A grim sense of satisfaction nudged its way into Amelia's brain as she pictured Julia Suarez-Moreno confronting her cheating husband. Murderer or not, Tim Moreno deserved everything headed his way. "Then we put a pin in Tim and Megan until we've got something to indicate their involvement. With everything we know about how the victims died, we can be confident we're looking for someone specific."

"Right. They'll not only have to be capable of the surgical

precision we've seen, but more than likely, they're going to be someone of means. More than just Tim Moreno and his embezzlement money." Dean gestured to a manila folder in the center of the table. "The M.E.'s report for Manning and Pendleton stated there were incisions that had started to heal, which means the perp didn't kill them right away. They also had marks around their wrists and ankles that indicated they struggled against some bindings. The other vics were more decomposed, but it's possible they had the same kinds of scars and healing wounds."

This line of thought had crossed Amelia's mind before, but she'd been too busy following up on Kent Manning's life circumstances to give it the consideration it deserved. "So what are you thinking? That the perp keeps these people alive while they gradually harvest their organs?"

Dean held out his hands, palms up. "That's what makes the most sense, don't you think? I did a little bit of reading last night after you guys all headed home, and apparently, most vital organ transplants take place when the donor is declared brain-dead. Human hearts can only last about six hours outside the body. There are some new methods of transportation being developed, but in most cases, six hours is the absolute maximum."

Amelia caught his implication. "Meaning if a heart is taken from a donor who's dead, then they have to rush to perform the transplant because the heart will no longer be usable after six hours. But if the donor is in a vegetative state, and their heart is still pumping, the doctors have more time to properly match it to someone on the waiting list, since the clock isn't ticking like it would be if the heart was already harvested."

"Exactly. I was thinking about the logistics of black-market organ sales. Most transactions in the industry are for kidneys, since they can last up to forty-eight hours outside the body, and because a person can donate a kidney and still survive. Hell, you can even donate a good portion of your liver. Did you know that livers regenerate? Because I didn't, until I went down this rabbit hole last night."

Despite the seriousness of the topic, Amelia enjoyed witnessing Dean's enthusiasm. He reminded her of a college student who'd just experienced a major breakthrough in one of their courses. "I did know that, but that's only because I binge watched all nine seasons of *House* when I was at the Boston Field Office."

Dean blew a quick raspberry. "I guess that's what I get for not watching medical dramas all these years." He waved a hand. "Anyway, the point of all that is, with how difficult it can be for legitimate channels to secure a heart or lung transplant, imagine how much more convoluted it has to be for someone operating outside the system. Outside the law."

"Well, organ traffickers are usually affiliated with a criminal organization. That way, they've got access to hospital staff who've been paid off or who're working with them already. They'd fudge the paper trail to make the entire thing look legitimate, which is why it's hard to get a bead on exactly how many illegal transplants occur in the United States."

Dean turned back to the dry-erase board. "True. But even then, wouldn't it be that much easier if they kept the vics alive until they had the details worked out for the transplant?"

Though Dean's logic made sense—too much sense—his implication painted a bleak picture. The idea of the Russian mob or one of the Mexican drug cartels keeping people comatose so they could harvest their organs one by one was truly the stuff of nightmares.

"It would, but it'd have to be incredibly expensive to pull it off. They'd need state-of-the-art medical equipment and people with the training and knowledge to use it. They'd basically have to have their own version of a hospital."

Dean leveled his index finger at Amelia like she'd won something. "They would, wouldn't they? And that kinda medical equipment ain't the type of stuff you just buy outta the back of ole Jimbo's van, you know?"

A light bulb lit up in Amelia's head. "Even when it comes to medical equipment manufacturers, there wouldn't be that many who make life support equipment. I suspect they'd have to be certified and approved by the government. If we start digging, maybe we can find private citizens who've made big purchases in the last year or two."

Before Dean could respond, blinds clattered against glass as the door swung open. Brown bag in hand, paper cup in the other, Zane stepped over the threshold, holding the door for Sherry. The faint aroma of fresh coffee and baked confections wafted past Amelia as Sherry closed the door behind them.

Zane held up the bag of pastries before setting it on the table, and Amelia's stomach grumbled. "Second breakfast is served."

Nudging Zane aside, Sherry placed a small, polka-dotted box beside the bag. "I didn't realize we were hobbits, but yes, second breakfast is served."

Zane swatted an invisible fly and took a seat at the end of the table. "You don't have to be a hobbit to enjoy second breakfast. I figure we've got a long day ahead of us, so we could use the sugar boost. Speaking of." His gray eyes shifted to Amelia, and then to Dean. "Did we miss anything while we were waiting in the drive-through for half our lives?"

As Sherry opened the donuts and passed around napkins, Amelia and Dean took turns recapping their discussion about high-grade medical equipment. Though Amelia was eager to begin the search for any private citizen or business who'd purchased life support machinery, she was just as keen on following up with the high school where Kent Manning had last been seen.

Considering Zane and Sherry had just sat in a car for nearly an hour to bring treats back to the office, Amelia and Dean volunteered to make the trip to the school. While they braved the abysmal Chicago traffic, Zane and Sherry took point on researching medical equipment providers.

A little over thirty minutes after departing the field office, Amelia and Dean pulled up to the front entrance of a sprawling, two-story building. The concrete exterior was slightly weathered, but still in good shape, and the driveway and parking lot were largely free of potholes. Even if Amelia hadn't already been familiar with the socioeconomic status of the neighborhood, the good repair of the school would've told her they were in one of the wealthier districts of Chicago.

"God, I don't miss having to come to one of these every day." Dean jerked a thumb at the entrance of the school as he killed the engine of their agency-issued black SUV.

Amelia didn't want to even think about those years. "Me neither. I'd rather come back as an FBI agent any day."

With a grin, Dean shoved open his door. The sunshine had taken most of the chill out of the morning air, but Amelia was still grateful she'd donned a light jacket for the trip.

A security guard greeted them just inside the entrance, and after showing the man their badges, they were waved past the metal detectors and directed to the school's main office. Fortunately, since they'd arrived between classes, there weren't many students out and about to gawk at them. They passed a pair of girls headed out of the office, but their eyes were glued firmly to Dean, leaving Amelia to wonder if they'd even noticed her.

Suppressing a chuckle, Amelia rapped on the doorframe before letting herself and Dean into the plainly furnished space.

Behind a sturdy wooden desk, a middle-aged man swiveled his chair away from a pair of computer monitors. He offered them a kind smile and readjusted his horn-rimmed glasses. "Good morning. How can I help you?"

Amelia smiled in return and flipped open her badge. "Hello, Mister..." she paused to make note of the secretary's silver nameplate, "Reasner. I'm Special Agent Storm and this is my partner, Special Agent Steelman."

On cue, Dean flashed his badge.

"We're investigating the murder of Kent Manning. He was a middle school teacher in this district, and our sources place him at this school before he disappeared." She rattled off the date and time Kent had gone missing, and the secretary perked up well before she'd finished.

"Mr. Manning, yes, I know him. The Chicago PD stopped by a week or so ago and spoke to my colleague." A distinct sadness tugged on the edges of Reasner's brown eyes. "Kent was a nice guy. He'd come by on weeknights to use the gym." Reasner held up a hand. "Let me take a look at the calendar. I think I was here on the night you mentioned for some school activity or another, but checking the calendar will jog my memory."

Resting his forearms on the tall desk, Dean nodded. "We appreciate it."

Though Amelia was grateful for the secretary's willingness to help, she wasn't exactly encouraged by the fact that the man had to look at a calendar to recall the night in question. Not that she faulted him for his lapse in memory—as far as he'd have been concerned, the evening would have been just another day. In a job like this, all the days undoubtedly blended together at some point.

Reasner tapped a few keys and leaned in closer to one of the monitors. "It looks like…yes. I was here that night." His face brightened and he snapped his fingers. "Right, I remember. It was a Wednesday, so the vendor was here to restock the vending machines. He and Kent got here at the same time, so it would've been right around six o'clock."

Amelia tempered her cautious optimism. "Do you remember Mr. Manning leaving? Was he with anyone then?"

Lips pursed, Reasner shook his head. "No. Jim, that's the vending guy, was gone in about half an hour. Kent left about another half hour after that. He was definitely alone, because I locked up the office and left at the same time."

Dean's jaw tensed. "Did he say anything about where he was going? Was he meeting anyone, going out to eat, anything at all?"

The secretary's shoulders slumped as if he'd just been deflated. "No. Just the usual 'see you tomorrow.'"

Amelia's positivity was gone as soon as it had appeared. "Are there any security cameras that might've caught him getting into his car or leaving?"

Another head shake. "We have security cameras for the parking lot in the front of the school, but the footage is automatically deleted on a rolling twenty-four-hour basis."

She wasn't surprised. Many surveillance systems made use of the same type of automatic deletion. "All right. Can you get us a list of anyone else who might've been working that night? We'd like to talk to them in case they saw something."

"Sure. Give me just a second and I'll print off the sign-in sheet and the janitorial schedule from that night."

"Thank you. We appreciate it."

As Amelia and Dean waited beside the desk, Amelia held back a sigh. One dead end had led them straight to yet another dead end.

She couldn't blame the overworked Chicago PD for not pulling the security cam footage from outside the school before it was deleted—the video had been deleted within a day.

Unfortunately, having a shot of Kent in the parking lot may have been quite useful. Chances were, they'd have caught the moment he was abducted. None of the other disappearances had been caught on camera, and now the one time they may have been caught, the footage was lost to them. Amelia couldn't believe their bad luck.

Dead end or not, Amelia would keep digging until she discovered who this sick bastard was.

19

Slumping down in the driver's seat of my car, I averted my gaze as the front door of a modest, ranch-style house swung open. Though I expected the man in the doorway to step out onto the porch, he simply stood in place. As another, more distant figure emerged, I sighed and rolled my eyes.

Hadn't I been patient enough already? Did I really have to sit out here and wait for these two imbeciles to run through another conversation about Spiderman?

Apparently, their evening had been spent playing an old video game, and they'd ended it by watching a film featuring the same superhero, Spiderman. Try as I might, I couldn't wrap my head around what drew grown adults to such juvenile entertainment. Bogdan had once brought up a superhero he liked, and it had taken a great deal of restraint for me to keep from rolling my eyes at him.

At the time, I hadn't known Bogdan as well as I did now. Upon realizing the man's brilliance in other areas, I'd allowed him a pass for his interest in such a pedantic topic.

As the men prattled on, I turned down the speaker

volume on my phone. A few months earlier, Bogdan had given me a mobile virus I could use to turn any smartphone into a constant bug. All I had to do was text a link to my target's phone, and I was in.

The tool had come in handy while I'd stalked Kari Hobill —listening to her conversations had helped greatly with detailing her routine. With all I'd learned by being a proverbial fly on the wall, I'd officially decided to make use of the technology for each of my upcoming patients.

To my dismay, this also meant sitting idly by while two morons discussed their grade-school-level interests.

I fought the urge to roll my eyes again. If I kept at it, I'd give myself vertigo. I needed my balance for what was coming tonight.

Like every other aspect of my research, I preferred my stalking to cause my patients as little distress as possible. I stuck to the shadows, monitored them from a distance, and only struck when I was certain I would succeed.

So far, not a single individual had gotten wise to my following them. As a result, I had yet to find myself in a position where I was forced to pursue a person.

I always wondered if the next subject would be the one to successfully put up a fight, but I didn't dwell on the topic to the point where it caused me concern. Even if the subject eluded me in a physical confrontation, I knew every little detail about their lives. There was no doubt in my mind that I'd get to them before they could go to the police.

Just as I was certain my quarry would never leave the doorway of this godforsaken house, the conversation shifted back to how the host had to work in the morning.

Thank God.

I slumped down a little more, preparing for the man to exit the house. Considering I was parked across the street and one house down, I doubted he'd spot me even if he was looking.

Regardless, engaging in stealth was half the fun of the chase. I'd disliked the so-called hunt at first, as I much preferred to have a specimen firmly in my grasp before I started to examine it. But thanks in part to Bogdan, I'd learned how much it was possible to discover while tailing my subjects.

Sure, I already knew plenty of hard facts—the quarry's blood type, weight, height, family medical history, personal medical history...and the list went on. But all that information only got me so far. What about their demeanor? I wanted to learn more about human resilience. What if there was a specific behavior associated with the individuals who could survive under harsher circumstances?

If I didn't thoroughly study my subjects, I'd never know.

I shook off the thoughts as the storm door swung open and my target stepped onto the covered porch.

"You've got a long drive home, my friend. That tire's not going to hold up for your entire trip." I chuckled at my clever machination.

This man was clueless. With the puncture I'd made to his tire, he'd be able to drive just far enough to get him away from the houses and potential onlookers of the city. He'd have no idea what hit him.

20

With a contented sigh, Lloyd Bishop melded into the heated seat. He shivered as he turned on the heat, silently begging the compressor to warm up faster.

Will and Lloyd had known one another for more than fourteen years—since they'd gone through college together. With a full-ride scholarship to the University of Illinois Chicago, Lloyd had uprooted from his home state and moved to Illinois. He'd never intended to stay in the Midwest, but Chicago and its abundance of culture had grown on him.

Waving to Will, Lloyd threw the truck into reverse. Beside the fuel gauge, he noted the red glow of the tire pressure icon.

No way, I just checked them a few days ago.

Pausing at the bottom of the drive, he squinted at the icon, as if his increased scrutiny would make it disappear.

The red glow only stared back.

Lloyd rubbed his tired eyes and blew out a sigh. Tire pressure gauges often displayed the warning after a drastic temperature change. Spring in the Midwest was dominated by wildly changing weather.

For example, the first few droplets of a surprise spring rain pattered the windshield.

With the weather having been thirty-two degrees only yesterday and now hovering near fifty, he reasoned the gauge was being finicky.

In the back of his mind, Lloyd knew he was searching for an excuse not to pull over at a gas station and manually check the tire pressure. Between the wind and now the rain, the last thing he wanted was to get out of his truck, hunch down near the wet ground, and fumble around with the tire.

He shook his head. "It's just the temperature change. It'll be fine. Now I just need to stop talking to myself like some kid rationalizing away the shadows in his bedroom."

Satisfied with the reasoning, he finally pulled out of Will's driveway and shifted the truck into drive.

Every other week, he and Will got together to hang out and catch up. Tonight, they'd spent the evening playing video games and watching one of the old Spiderman films they'd obsessed over in college.

The drive to visit Will took Lloyd up north and out of the city, but he didn't mind the extra time on the road. It normally gave him a chance to decompress after a long work week.

Normally.

As the welcoming glow of the streetlights faded in the rearview mirror, the little hairs on the back of Lloyd's neck rose to attention. For the first time that night, the cold wasn't to blame for the series of goose bumps. Transitioning from the well-lit streets of the little town to the relative darkness of the stretch of road leading back to Chicago was always a bit eerie, especially considering how accustomed Lloyd had become to the constant lights and sounds of Chicago.

Houses gave way to the dark, skeletal husks of trees clustered beside the road, the occasional gap forming where a driveway led to a relatively secluded house, cabin, or business. Though the view of Lake Michigan was obscured, Lloyd knew the massive body of water wasn't far off the road.

Living this close to nature would've been cool if it wasn't so damn creepy.

What's that?

Lloyd's pulse thumped as he stared into the rearview mirror. He could've sworn there'd been movement back there—a dark shape cruising along the road behind him.

Who in the hell would be driving through the rain without their headlights on, though?

No one. That's who. You're seeing things. It might've been a deer crossing the road, or someone pulling out of their driveway.

Rubbing the back of his neck, Lloyd let out a nervous laugh. "What am I even worried about, anyway? Bigfoot? The boogeyman? Maybe the Jersey Devil is on vacation, doing some fishing at Lake Michigan."

Come on. You're nice and warm in the cabin of your truck. The seat warmer is on full blast, they're talking about ducks on the radio, and you've only got another half hour before you're home.

Perhaps he was still squeamish to drive on an isolated road in the rain after he'd hydroplaned and wrecked his old car last fall. The accident was a nasty one, with Lloyd busting his nose so badly he'd been referred to a plastic surgeon's office to fix it. Fortunately, only he and a concrete median had been involved, and aside from his nose, he'd made it out mostly unscathed.

That had to be it. Maybe he had a mild form of post-traumatic stress that made him imagine obstacles on the road behind him.

Or is someone following me?

Lloyd's stomach tied itself in knots as his palms went clammy.

What the hell was going on? Was he about to have a panic attack, or was his brain trying to tell him something?

It's a panic attack. It's got to be. Will deals with these things all the time. What did he say he does when he gets one? He counts things?

Christ, Lloyd couldn't remember. His chest was growing tighter, and his grip on the steering wheel had become vise-like. Even if he wanted to loosen his grasp, he wasn't sure he was capable of doing so.

Suddenly, the excuses he'd given himself not to check his tires were the worst idea he'd had in recent memory. His evening had gone from good to shit in record time.

No, don't think about that. Come on, what does Will do when he has a panic attack? Counts things he can see or something like that?

"Well, I can see the fucking tire pressure icon." Lloyd spat the words more than spoke them. "Then there's the boogeyman I keep seeing in my rearview mirror."

Come on, Lloyd. That's not how you do that. You're acting like a baby.

Still maintaining his death grip on the wheel, Lloyd took in a long, loud breath. He counted to three and exhaled. "All right. What are some things I can see? Uh, well, there's the air freshener. How long have I even had this thing? Does it even have a smell anymore?"

Dammit. He was doing it wrong again.

"Um, let's see, there's the road, obviously. And they're still talking about ducks on NPR, but I guess I can't see that."

This was useless. He couldn't keep himself focused enough on the task to count more than two items.

Despite his inability to follow through on what he thought Will did to calm himself down during an anxiety attack, a sliver of tension had already begun to seep out of Lloyd's tired muscles.

He was being ridiculous. Odds were his sudden bout of panic had to do with memories of the accident that had ruined his nose.

Everything was fine. He was warm, the seat warmer was still functioning, ducks had highly waterproof feathers. As long as his tire didn't—

He hadn't finished the thought when the truck began to jostle up and down like he'd just turned onto the roughest terrain on the planet. Of the many vehicles Lloyd had owned throughout his life, he'd only driven on a flat once before, but he sure as hell hadn't forgotten the signs.

"Son of a bitch!" He thumped the steering wheel with the palm of his hand.

The same panic from moments earlier threatened to rise up and consume his rational mind, and Lloyd spat out a series of four-letter words.

"No. We're not doing this again, brain. I can change a tire. I've helped plenty of people change tires over the years. I'll change it, go home, and deal with the rest of this shit tomorrow."

He wasn't pleased about the idea of traipsing around in the cold rain, but his sudden irritation chased away the hesitancy.

Flicking on his hazard lights, Lloyd eased his foot down on the brake and pulled as far onto the shoulder as he could without risking a tumble into the muddy ditch. With the soft *tink, tink, tink* of the hazards barely audible over the radio commercial, Lloyd leaned back against the headrest, suddenly exhausted. For a long moment, his eyelids drooped closed, blocking out the background world.

The glow of a new light source pierced through his closed lids, and when his first thought was that he was about to be abducted by aliens, an unflattering chortle slipped from his lips.

Blinking repeatedly, Lloyd straightened in his seat. Rather than the beam of a UFO, the new source of illumination was the headlights of a fellow motorist who'd pulled up behind Lloyd's truck.

A good Samaritan, or is this Bigfoot's car?

"Stop it."

As someone who'd pulled over to help stranded drivers in the past, Lloyd was grateful for the presence of another human being. Changing a tire wasn't difficult, but the glow of the other car's headlights would make the task even easier.

Killing the engine, Lloyd pocketed his keys and hopped out onto the wet asphalt.

Silhouette cutting through the twin beams, a middle-aged man with short dark hair and a black peacoat waved one gloved hand in greeting. "Evening, friend. Looks like you're having a bit of car trouble, eh?"

A flush heated Lloyd's cheeks, and he was grateful for the relatively low light. "Flat tire. I'm not sure what happened to it, but I've got a spare."

The man raised an eyebrow. "Anything I can do to help?"

"Actually," Lloyd gestured to the stranger's car, "just keeping your headlights on my truck is a huge help. Then I don't have to try to juggle a flashlight while I do this."

Grinning, the man flashed him a thumbs-up. "Looks like it's your rear passenger tire. I noticed it as I was pulling up behind you here."

"Really? Thanks. Let me take a look at it." As Lloyd circled around the truck, the man stepped out of his way.

Sure enough, the flattened tire was plainly visible in the harsh glow of the other car's headlights. Holding back yet another sigh, Lloyd crouched down beside the truck to get a closer look at the damage. He didn't have the first clue how his tire would have been punctured while just sitting idly in Will's driveway, but as the saying went, stranger things had happened.

Rubbing his clammy hands on his jeans, Lloyd nodded. "Yeah, looks like that tire's pretty well done for. I'll take it to a shop and see if they can patch it, but I think I might be stuck having to get a new one altogether."

"That's a shame." The stranger's voice was far closer than Lloyd had realized, and he nearly jumped out of his skin at the unexpected proximity.

As he began to pivot in his crouch to face the man, he barely registered a blur of motion in the corner of his eye, followed by a sharp sting in the side of his neck.

"What the hell?" Clamping one hand over the site of the... whatever the hell it was, Lloyd spun around and managed to get to his feet just in time to see the stranger recapping a hypodermic needle. "What...did you just..." His tongue was suddenly thick and cumbersome as he tried to form the next words in his query.

Swallowing, as if the gesture would help him regain his ability to speak, Lloyd stumbled backward a step and barely caught himself on the tailgate of his truck.

His vision turned to liquid as the world around him flickered like a dying light bulb.

"There, there, Lloyd." The stranger's calm voice cut through the turmoil in Lloyd's body and mind. It should have struck him as bizarre that the man knew his name when he'd not mentioned even one detail about himself, but he didn't have the energy to scrutinize the interaction anymore.

He was tired, cold, and...drunk? No, he'd been drugged. With what?

Don't just fall over. Do something! This crazy bastard just stabbed you with a syringe!

Adrenaline rushed through Lloyd's veins, but the reaction

was too little and too late. Lloyd wasn't sure when, but at some point, he'd fallen backward onto his ass. The gravel beneath him dug into his skin, but he hardly felt the stabbing rocks.

He was too disoriented to mount a counterattack. Maybe if he closed his eyes and rested for a beat, he could get his bearings and fight back against…against what?

Lloyd didn't have a chance to ponder the answer to the question as he slumped down to the cold, wet ground.

21

As had become the norm, Amelia was the first back to the incident room after the team's lunch break. Zane and Dean had gone to Herman's Sandwich Shop while Amelia had opted for Thai. Though she was a fan of Herman's, she wasn't obsessed with the place quite like Zane and Dean. In the week since she and Dean had visited the high school where Kent Manning was last seen, Zane and Dean had grabbed lunch from Herman's four times.

Though Amelia and the others had put their collective noses to the grindstone in their search for the perp responsible for killing at least five people and stealing their organs, they hadn't made much progress. The killer was elusive, and trace evidence from each victim was minimal at best. For the most part, all the lab had to analyze was the gauze and plastic wrap that had covered the gaping chest wound of each corpse.

Taking a long drink of her lemonade, Amelia leaned back in her chair as the door swung inward to reveal none other than Dean and Zane.

"Welcome back, gentlemen. How was Herman's today?"

Zane grinned and took his seat at the table. While they awaited the return of Sherry and Layton, along with the Organized Crime SSA, Spencer Corsaw, they chatted about what they'd ordered for lunch.

Amelia was unsurprised to learn Zane had eaten the same Philly cheesesteak sandwich he'd fallen in love with a week ago. According to him, Herman's made a proper Philly by using processed cheese sauce instead of melting a piece of actual cheese on it. The concoction sounded like a heart attack on a bun to Amelia, but she assured Zane she'd try it one of these days. Maybe.

Once Sherry and Spencer filed into the incident room, the mood swung back to the usual air of professionalism. Layton Redker was only a couple of minutes behind, a half-eaten donut in one hand and a coffee in the other.

Arms crossed over his black suit jacket, Spencer leaned against the wall beside the window. Even with the shades drawn, plenty of the sun's warm glow made its way into the room. "All right, Agents. Thanks for humoring me with this briefing. It's been about a week since I last touched base with you, so let's see where we've gotten in that time."

Holding in a sigh, Amelia propped her elbows on the table. "This past week has been mostly follow-up on each of the victims' final days. We reinterviewed friends and family members to see if they'd remember anything now that some time had passed, but it didn't lead to anything promising. And we revisited all the victims' last known whereabouts."

Spencer's gaze was on the dry-erase board as he nodded his understanding. "What about common threads between the victims? Is there anything that could tie any of them to traffickers of any kind?"

Zane stretched both arms in front of himself. "That's the angle we've been working on, but it hasn't shown any promise either. As far as we can tell, all our vics were normal folks who lived normal lives. There are a few common threads that we've noticed, such as their age, overall health, and the fact that none of them had any kids. Kent Manning was the only one who was married."

Rubbing his chin, Spencer's gaze swept over the five of them. Though the SSA was still in the process of stepping down to the role of a field agent, Amelia appreciated his leadership style. She'd never been struck by the notion that Spencer regarded himself in a different light than the agents he managed, and she respected him for it.

Finally, Spencer pulled out a chair. "What do you make of those commonalities, Redker? Not to put you on the spot, but the lack of physical evidence and witnesses means the BAU is going to be our biggest asset right now."

Layton wiped his fingers on a napkin, his donut now completely gone. "We've established that the killer is someone with means, and a high level of education to boot. It's hard to say if he had means because he started selling organs on the black market, or if he's always had means. Either way, he has to have the finances to maintain a facility with life support for these victims."

"Right." Spencer scooted toward the table. "The M.E.'s report stated the tox screens turned up substances consistent with general anesthesia."

"And a fresh scar on Kent Manning indicates he'd been kept alive for an extended time as each organ was removed and sold." Zane gave Amelia a look for confirmation.

She nodded in agreement.

Rolling his chair back, Dean rapped his knuckles on the whiteboard. "And there were multiple incisions on each vic's body. The M.E. wasn't quite sure what all of them were for, since there were some on the neck and the insides of their legs. Dr. Francis thinks it might be for the form of life support the perp was using."

Spencer's expression darkened, and Amelia couldn't blame him. The victims' final days had been ripped straight out of a horror film. "So this guy is keeping these people alive while he harvests their organs?"

Dean lifted a shoulder and let it fall. "That's what the evidence suggests."

"Where's Cyber at on tracking dark web organ sales around the area?"

As he tossed his napkin, Layton shook his head. "Not much luck. My old partner in Cyber is one of the agents working on it. He said they were close to pinning down something a few days ago, but they lost it when the forum disappeared. There's some good news with that, though. Next time more of this activity pops up, they'll have a good idea of where to start looking. Unfortunately, that means it's just a matter of time."

In this case, "a matter of time" meant waiting for another victim. Amelia hated the idea, but they were at an impasse. They needed more evidence, and there was only one way to get it.

"All right, that's good, Redker." Spencer turned to Amelia and Sherry. "Has any progress been made in tracking down the sale of life-saving equipment to private individuals?"

Shifting in her seat, Amelia addressed the SSA. "When our search didn't turn up anything, Dean and I asked Cyber to follow that trail of bread crumbs. So far, they haven't unearthed anything either."

Spencer rubbed his chin. "How about the Tim Moreno angle? Has there been any activity there? Maybe an indication Moreno's a fan of the dark web?"

Amelia had been keeping tabs on Tim Moreno and Megan Manning as closely as she was legally allowed, but neither of them had turned into a viable lead. "Nothing. Tim Moreno's wife is filing for divorce, and Megan Manning listed her and Kent's house for sale, but nothing suspicious has cropped up. We've looked over Moreno's schedule during the approximate times of death for the other victims, and he was out of town when two of them occurred. His whereabouts are accounted for when Kent Manning disappeared, as well as when he was killed."

At Amelia's side, Zane lifted a finger, silently drawing the room's attention to him. "I've gone through records of transplants as well as I can, considering HIPAA, but there's a lot of red tape between us and that information."

Spencer let out a sound akin to a grunt. "Yeah, that's what I figured. I have a friend who works in one of the major transplant hospitals in the city. I reached out to him the other day to ask what he knew about organ trafficking, but he's an oncologist. Let me reach out again, see if I can persuade him to keep his ear to the ground for me."

The suggestion was a long shot to Amelia, but at this point, long shots were better than nothing.

"I did the same, actually." Sherry gave Spencer a hapless shrug. "But my friend didn't know anything either. If I had to guess, I'd say the hospital staff involved in that sort of thing keep it quiet. My friend said that any staff with a stake in organ sales would probably forge information, starting with the agency that manages the acquisition of organs for transplant. But like Palmer already said, that's going to be coated in red tape. All those agencies prefer to keep the identities of their donors a secret, even for a legitimate transplant."

"Right. I've got a meeting with SAC Keaton later today, so let me see if she can lean on anyone involved in the process." With another gander at the dry-erase board, Spencer flattened a palm against the table and shoved to his feet. "I hate to say it, but keep doing what you're doing. We're being as thorough as we possibly can, which is all we can do at this point."

Amelia and the others bade Spencer farewell, assuring the SSA they'd update him if any new developments occurred.

Though she realized Spencer was right, the statement didn't make Amelia feel any less pessimistic. Time was of the essence in murder cases, and a week had already passed during which they'd learned…what, exactly?

Nothing. None of the victims knew one another, and they hadn't even lived in the same zip codes. We know they were all healthy, but that just makes sense when we're dealing with an organ trafficker.

Amelia gave herself a mental shake. The negativity was no surprise when she'd been running into one dead end after another, but she needed to get rid of the sentiment. As she went for another drink of lemonade, her disappointment compounded on realizing the cup was empty.

I'm not going to sulk just because I'm still thirsty. Find a solution, don't wallow.

There were vending machines scattered throughout the field office, and plenty of them stocked bottled lemonade. A short walk outside the incident room would no doubt be beneficial for her mental health as well.

Snatching a credit card out of her handbag, Amelia rose to her feet. "I'll be right back."

Zane offered her a reassuring smile as he pushed open his laptop, and Sherry gave a thumbs-up.

Stepping out into the hall, Amelia stretched her back and rolled her shoulders before setting off for the break area. She'd taken a grand total of four steps when her cell buzzed in the pocket of her striped cardigan.

"I swear, if this is about my car's extended warranty again…" She left the threat unfinished as she retrieved the device and checked the screen.

To her pleasant surprise, the caller was the medical examiner's office.

Hope rose in Amelia's chest as she swiped the screen. "This is Agent Storm."

"Agent Storm, good afternoon. This is Dr. Francis." The forensic pathologist's tone was as kind as always, but Amelia detected a slight strain in the greeting.

Amelia tempered her enthusiasm before responding. "Afternoon, Dr. Francis. What can I help you with?"

"Well, I just received a call from my colleague in Kendall County, just a county over southwest of Cook County. The sheriff's department out there just found the body of a woman with gauze and plastic wrap covering her chest, and several smaller incisions in different locations. She also has ligature marks around her wrists and ankles."

Amelia's enthusiasm quickly morphed into grim determination. "I see. Is the body on its way to Cook County, then?"

"It is. Jane Doe should be here within the hour, and we'll get to work on identifying her and conducting the post-mortem exam. I wanted to let you know as soon as I found out, so you and your partner could come by and see for yourselves."

"Thank you. Let me know as soon as she's there and we'll head your way."

After saying their farewells, Amelia killed the call and shoved her phone back into her pocket.

She hadn't wanted to rely on another victim to find their lead, but as long as they were here, she'd do her damnedest to make sure her death wasn't in vain.

If the killer slipped up, Amelia would be ready.

22

A renewed sense of purpose propelled Amelia forward as she and Dean Steelman exited the fortress-like medical examiner's office. When they'd first arrived, their primary concern had been identifying the body of their most recent victim. To Amelia's relief, a few aspects from the newest victim's murder had worked in their favor.

First and most importantly, according to Dr. Francis, the woman had barely been dead for twelve hours when her body was found. Her corpse was easily the least decomposed of the six they'd discovered thus far, which made locating identifying information significantly easier.

Secondly, and almost as importantly as the state of decomposition, the woman's fingerprints had been in the system. Kari Hobill, age thirty, had worked as a social worker for Cook County since she'd graduated with her master's in social work at twenty-five. During graduate school, she'd done an internship at the Cook County Jail, at which time her prints had been entered into the national database.

As Amelia climbed into the passenger seat of the black SUV, Dean took his place behind the wheel.

Turning the key over in the ignition, Dean shot her a curious look. "Cowen and Palmer are at the site where Hobill's body was found. Any word from either of them?"

Amelia double-checked her phone, but there were no new notifications. "Not yet. I doubt they'll find much at the site anyway."

"True." Dean shifted the SUV into gear and backed out of the parking space. "Dr. Francis said Hobill's body was just as clean as the others, so the same's probably true for the dump site."

Pulling a tablet out of her handbag, Amelia turned on the device. Kari Hobill's father lived in a quiet suburb west of Chicago, and in the middle of the afternoon, they'd have plenty of time to do a review of Kari's background.

As Amelia tapped and scrolled in the relative silence of the SUV, she couldn't help but notice Dean's impatient drumming on the steering wheel.

He's dealing with Chicago traffic with no radio on, so he's probably going insane.

Amelia could sympathize with his plight. The least she could do was narrate her findings, mundane though they might be. "Let's see, Kari Hobill, age thirty, social worker for Cook County for the last five years. She recently moved from Hyde Park out to the 'burbs after a divorce."

One of Dean's eyebrows quirked up. "A divorce?"

"Yep. Finalized six months ago. Her ex-husband lives in… California. He moved out there around the same time Kari moved to the Shady Oak suburb."

Dean snorted. "Sounds like a retirement home."

Despite the grim situation, Amelia chuckled. "I won't argue that. Otherwise, Kari's record is squeaky clean. She's never pressed charges in court, never even had a speeding ticket. Worked for the state since she graduated, and…that's about it. No kids, same as the others."

"You know, when you think about it, it's kinda weird." He glanced at Amelia, then back at the road as they neared an on-ramp for the interstate. "Your run-of-the-mill organ traffickers target migrants and transient folks, right?"

"Right. The same types of high-risk individuals serial killers tend to target."

"That's true. Plenty of serials will use prostitutes or homeless folks as a twisted form of training. Preparing themselves to go after a different demographic." He waved a hand. "But that's a little different from this perp, though it's possible he could've started by hunting victims from higher-risk demographics. Now he targets middle-class people working office jobs, but he seems to make sure none of them have kids or spouses. Someone who'd quickly report them missing, and who'd make a fuss right from the get-go."

"He's selective." Amelia was intrigued by the pattern, but at this point, she wasn't sure what good the observation would do them. "How is that significant, though? More than likely, it's a simple explanation. He wants his victims healthy since he's harvesting and selling their organs."

Dean tapped his thumbs on the steering wheel. "What if he's not selling them, though? What if he's just cutting these folks apart because he's some kind of mad scientist? Some rich guy who's got more money than he knows what to do with, and he's decided to use a substantial portion of it to... hell, I don't know. To make his own Frankenstein? To see how long it takes to dissolve a human heart in a jar of acid?"

Dean's suggestion painted an even more horrific picture of the killer in Amelia's mind. As Zane was fond of reminding her, greed was an easy motive to understand. Too often, the pursuit of power and money led otherwise normal, law-abiding citizens down a path of treachery and violence.

What about those who were propelled by an entirely different goal? Though Amelia was well-versed in the organized crime landscape of Chicago, she wasn't as familiar with the criminal world's outliers—the murderers who hovered on the fringe, who pureed their victims' eyeballs into a new shade of paint.

They were unfamiliar to her, but she wanted to learn more.

For the remainder of the drive, she perused Kari Hobill's social media, rattling off her findings to keep Dean from losing his mind.

As Dean pulled the SUV up in front of a beige, two-story home with an attached garage, Amelia double-checked the house number to ensure they'd stopped at the right place. Aside from the varying shades of beige and gray, she could barely tell the houses apart.

Tucking away her tablet and handbag, Amelia stepped out into the temperate spring breeze. The scent of fresh-cut grass drifted down the street, a welcome reprieve from what she was used to in the city.

Amelia fell in beside Dean as they made their way along the sidewalk to a small covered porch. Before they'd hit the first step, the front door swung inward. The man in the entryway looked as if he hadn't slept in close to a week. His face was scruffy, his t-shirt wrinkled, and dark circles hovered beneath his green eyes.

He opened the screen door, and despite his beleaguered appearance, his gaze was shrewd as he glanced from Dean to Amelia. "You must be Agents Storm and Steelman. Come on in."

Stepping over the threshold, Amelia flipped open her badge for good measure. "Thanks for speaking with us so quickly, Mr. Hobill."

"Mm-hmm. Barrett is fine." Barrett peeked at Amelia's badge and then Dean's. "You said my daughter is dead. Is that true?"

For the second time, his blunt query set Amelia a bit off-balance.

"I'm afraid so." Dean tucked his badge back into the interior pocket of his suit jacket. "We've confirmed her identity via fingerprint analysis. She's with the Cook County medical examiner right now."

The bereaved man raked a hand through his brown-and-silver hair. "I knew it. When they didn't find her after I reported her missing, I knew it. I knew they'd never find her alive." His eyes turned glassy as he looked away. "I'm sure you'll have some questions for me. Come on, we can talk in the living room."

Amelia and Dean followed Barrett down a short hall to a large, sunlit space complete with a sectional sofa, coffee table, matching end tables, and a television that was at least sixty inches. The living area was open to the kitchen, allowing the aroma of garlic and onions to waft over to them as they sat on the couch.

"Thank you again for talking to us on such short notice." Dean's tone was gentler than Amelia had even suspected possible from a guy who looked like he'd just strolled out of a noir crime film. "My partner and I are very sorry for your loss."

Jaw tightening, Barrett nodded once. "Thank you. I'll do whatever I can to help you, but I'm not sure I'll have any useful information. Kari and I were close, but we're both... boring, for lack of a better term."

Amelia gave the poor guy a reassuring smile as she pulled a small notebook and pen from her cardigan. "That's all right. We noticed Kari was divorced within the past year. It wasn't contentious, at least on paper. What could you tell us about Kari's relationship with her ex-husband?"

Barrett sighed, his shoulders slumping. "Clint Haney. He was, is, a decent guy. Their relationship didn't work out because they both sort of…grew apart, is how Kari put it. It was about as amicable a divorce as I've ever seen, and I've had plenty of friends get divorced over the years. Clint moved to California afterward, and Kari moved out here to Shady Oak."

As Amelia jotted down the information, Dean took over. "Do you know of anyone who might've wanted to hurt Kari? Had she mentioned a disgruntled client from work, maybe a parent who was upset about the state's involvement in their family, that sort of thing?"

Barrett fidgeted with his silver wedding band. "No. My… my wife was a social worker, too, before she passed. So Kari would talk to me about work when she came over to visit, but she didn't ever mention anyone being out to get her."

Dean folded his hands on his lap. "When was the last time you saw Kari?"

"She stopped by for dinner on Friday, two weeks ago. She sent me a few texts during the day on Saturday, but then I didn't hear anything from her on Sunday. She's a grown woman, though, so I didn't pester her." He paused to rub his temples. "Then, on Monday, her boss called me and said she hadn't shown up to work. She'd tried to get ahold of Kari, but all the calls were going straight to voicemail. That's when I went over to her house to check on her. And she…she was gone."

Amelia made a note to have the crime scene unit go through Kari's home. "Was anything in her house out of place? Any signs of a struggle, things like that?"

"No." Barrett sighed. "Nothing. Kari kept her space pretty tidy, and it didn't look like anything had been touched. I didn't see her phone anywhere, and her car keys were gone. The cops found her car at Casey Park a couple days later. She'd go there to run."

The recollection had begun to paint a grim picture of

Kari's final hours. Like all the previous victims, she'd gone out for a routine activity and had simply vanished. Kent Manning's car had been located in the high school lot where he'd last been seen, and Murphy Pendleton's truck had been found on a residential street not far from where he'd lived.

Like the Manning and Pendleton cases, the Bureau would take custody of Kari's vehicle and search it thoroughly for any trace of a suspicious third party. If Kari's situation was similar to Manning's and Pendleton's, though, the lab would find nothing. Honestly, Amelia doubted the perp even bothered to touch the victims' vehicles.

So far, the modi operandi were exactly the same.

Setting aside the thoughts, Amelia cleared her throat. "Barrett, do you mind if we have our forensic specialists search your daughter's home?"

"Not at all. I have a spare set of keys you can use, so you won't have to go through the property owner. Look through whatever you need, for as long as you need. If you need my permission to examine anything, you've got it. Just let me know." For a moment, his melancholy was replaced with a flicker of rage. "Just do whatever you have to do to catch the son of a bitch who killed my little girl."

23

Saul Avery had finally admitted defeat. Shifting against the mound of pillows propping up his back, he stared absently at the flickering television screen mounted to the wall, his hand resting over his failing heart. With a sigh, he slumped down a little deeper into the cushiony mattress, smoothing out the blankets over his lap as he did.

He'd resisted the move to the first-floor guest room for as long as he could—too long—but two days earlier, he'd asked Mandy to help relocate all the medical equipment from their bedroom upstairs to the guest room. Though he'd fully intended to help her, she'd shot him a fiery warning glare at the suggestion. The look wasn't one he witnessed often, but when he saw it, he knew better than to continue his display of obstinance.

As much as he hated to admit it, the transition downstairs had been for the best. Saul's strength was waning a little more as each day passed, and he knew he wasn't long for this world. If he was alone, he'd have already made peace with the fact that he was going to die.

But he wasn't alone. His wife's love for him was plainly

visible in her face whenever she looked at him. They'd been through so much over the years, not to mention the horrors she'd endured before he'd even met her. Saul had grown up in a stable, middle-class home, but Mandy's childhood was marked by multiple forms of abuse and trauma that had followed her into her adult years.

Because of her upbringing and early career choices, Saul's family hated her. His siblings had referred to her as *trailer trash*. And his parents? Before they'd bitten the dust, they'd made their stance on Saul's wife quite clear. Not only had she been unwelcome at their family gatherings, but she and Saul had been prohibited from collecting anything from their estate when they died.

The joke was on them, though. Saul had busted his ass in the world of real estate, and he'd made more money than his folks or siblings could've ever dreamed.

Now, when he died, none of them would see a dime. His entire fortune, created with the constant support of the one person Saul loved most in this world, would go to the woman his family had shunned. The petty part of him hoped Mandy would rub their faces in it.

Shaking himself out of the contemplation, Saul realized he'd begun to drift off.

He pushed himself farther up onto the throne of pillows —Mandy's term, which made him chuckle every time she said it—and rubbed his eyes. "This bed is *too* comfortable. I'm going to need to lie on the floor if I ever want to finish watching anything without falling asleep."

"I heard that!"

As Mandy's voice drifted in from the hall, an involuntary smile crept over Saul's face. "I'm not serious, all right? It's a wooden floor. It'd be *so* uncomfortable."

With a light laugh, his wife emerged in the open doorway. Though she was normally a sharp dresser, her t-shirt and capri sweats had become something of a staple in her time away from work.

Gesturing at the television, Mandy padded over the hardwood and took a seat at the edge of the bed. "You're still not done with this movie? When did you start watching it?" Her tone wasn't accusatory, but it struck Saul as more bemused than anything. It might have been wishful thinking on his part, but he could have sworn she was…lighter. Happier. Maybe even a little hopeful.

He offered her a grin and a shrug. "I told you, this bed is too comfortable. I keep falling asleep while I'm trying to watch it."

They both knew the real reason Saul was asleep so often these days. His body was failing him, his heart preparing to throw in the towel.

Saul was confident the thought must have occurred to her, but to his surprise, her smile didn't falter. "I've got some good news."

The announcement piqued his curiosity. "About?"

She reached out to tap his sternum, her touch light as a feather. "A donor."

A mixture of optimism and tentative dread roiled in Saul's gut. "A donor? You mean…a heart, right? Does that mean someone died?"

Her expression softened as she rubbed his shoulder. "Yeah. The person I've been in touch with, the seller, says this man suffered some sort of accident. He wouldn't give me any specifics, probably because he doesn't want me to figure out who the donor is." She paused and wrinkled her nose. "But the point is, he says the man had an accident that's left him brain-dead. He's hooked up to life support right now, but, well…"

Sadness dampened Saul's sliver of hope. He wouldn't let himself forget they were talking about a human being—

someone's son, brother, maybe even father. Stealing a dead person's organs was new territory for Saul, but he was determined to maintain respect for the dead.

He turned back to Mandy. "He's not there anymore. The person he was is gone, right?"

She offered him a sad smile. "Right. He's not registered as an organ donor either. But this person I'm in contact with has contacts who can change that. The blood type is a match, and so is the size. All we have to do now is offer him more money than the next person in line."

As Mandy squeezed his hand, her eyes alight with a hopefulness he hadn't witnessed in months, Saul would have paid anything to ensure she was happy. If that meant handing over a small fortune to steal the heart of a dead man so he'd have a few more years on this planet, then Saul would do it.

He gingerly wrapped his fingers around hers, forcing a reassuring smile onto his face. "All right. I trust you, honey. I know you know what you're dealing with. Whatever the price is, we can afford it."

A tidbit of doubt remained in Saul's heart, but he ignored the nagging sensation as Mandy wrapped her arms around his shoulders in a tight embrace.

Whatever the price, he'd pay it.

Right?

24

As I reached for the mug on the table beside my recliner, I was disappointed to find it empty. Pushing in the footrest, I set my book facedown on the arm of the chair and glanced toward the kitchen. The digital clock beneath the television told me it was already five in the evening, though I had no earthly idea where the time had gone. I could have sworn it was only two when I'd last checked.

Mug in hand, I rose to my feet. With the hour suddenly so late, I most certainly didn't need more caffeine. A glass of water would have to suffice.

After procuring my drink, I snatched my laptop off the dining room table and took it back to the recliner. I'd taken most of the afternoon off work—both my day job and my *dream* job—but I could never stay away for too long.

Powering on the computer, I scooped up *Ethan Frome* and set it on the nearby coffee table. Amusement lifted my spirits as I recalled my most recent literary discussion with Bogdan. My Russian friend was as intelligent as they came, so his disdain for classic novels had taken me by surprise. Reading timeless works of literature was my favorite pastime, and I particularly enjoyed Bogdan's least favorite book, *Moby Dick*.

I chuckled as I kicked up my feet. "Maybe someday your tastes will mature, my friend. I'll let you have a look through my collection once you're here in the States."

The sense of amusement lingered as I pulled up a web browser to check the local news. A little more than a day had elapsed since I'd removed Kari's heart and dumped her body outside the city. I'd have preferred to travel a bit farther south to an even more rural area, but I sincerely doubted the cops were onto me. If they hadn't caught on by now, I was certain I could continue to elude them indefinitely.

Besides, even if the location I'd selected was closer to the city than usual, it was still in no way tied to me. Forensics wasn't my expertise, but I was certain the bodies of all my patients were free of trace evidence. Each of them was kept in a sterile location for the entirety of their stay. There was no chance I'd transferred a fiber or a hair or any of that other nonsense.

The reason I checked the news wasn't because I was worried the cops would show up on my doorstep. Honestly, I enjoyed witnessing the reactions of the newscasters when they discussed my patients. I'd had a difficult time admitting it to myself at first, but these days, I'd made peace with my morbid curiosity.

As I navigated to a local news site, excitement prickled my scalp. A grainy image of a handful of sheriff's deputies gathered near a creek bed was captioned with *Kendall County sheriff's deputies follow up on the discovery of a woman's body in a local farmer's pasture.*

Amused, I skimmed through the article. The reporter speculated on a link between Kari and some other bodies discovered in rural northern Illinois, but apparently, the investigators assigned to the cases weren't all that forthcoming with details. When I spotted the name of the man the writer had tried to contact, I understood why.

"Supervisory Special Agent? So the sheriffs' departments handed their cases over to the Feds, did they? The Bureau has always been secretive about what they work on behind the scenes. They aren't going to give out too many details right now because they don't want the citizens to start panicking. Not that I'd go after just anyone."

Most Illinois residents had nothing to worry about. I was quite selective, and with good reason. My work in a plastic surgeon's office gave me access to the records of men and women who were otherwise healthy, and from there, I only picked those who matched my strict criteria.

I exited the news site and opened my real web browser. Earlier in the day, I'd communicated with a prospective buyer who was very interested in Lloyd Bishop's heart. From what I'd gathered in our discussion, they were of substantial means.

More importantly, they were desperate.

Now, money wasn't what motivated me to continue this work, but I certainly needed funds to keep the operation afloat. I'd received contact from another similarly frantic buyer in the past, and the deal had been quite lucrative.

Unsurprisingly, as I went about checking on the auctions for Lloyd's organs, I had received a new message from the interested buyer.

They'd provided me with a new bid, and I stared in shock at the number of zeroes.

"A million." I blinked repeatedly, but the figure didn't change. "A million dollars? Two, if I can facilitate the sale within the next two days. Well, I sure wish I knew who in the hell I'm dealing with here. But if the money is there, then far be it from me to deny the request."

This buyer's insistence on buying Lloyd's heart within the next couple of days threw off my entire routine.

But *two million*? How could I say no to so much money? The most I'd made off the sale of a heart in the past was six hundred thousand. With two million, I could purpose and conceal a crematorium, which would eliminate the risky business of body dumps.

How would I maintain the health of Lloyd's remaining organs in the absence of his heart, though? Sure, the ECMO machine I used was a miracle of modern technology, but a person still needed a heart for it to work.

With my gaze fixed on the screen, I ran through my options.

The auctions on Lloyd's other organs were all still open— two kidneys, two lungs, and two pieces of his liver. Any other parts of Lloyd were sold by request only, and at my strict discretion.

Maybe if I worked quickly, I could still secure all six additional sales and meet the time frame provided by the buyer interested in Lloyd's heart.

I made note of the date in the bottom corner of my screen.

Dammit. Today was Friday, which meant my colleague expected me at work tomorrow. Damn him and his Saturday procedures. *"It's more convenient for some folks. It's good for business."* I scoffed every time he uttered that drivel.

I coughed into my hand. "Well, it's a shame I feel like I'm coming down with something."

Though I needed my job to make my real business that much easier, I was confident I wouldn't be fired for calling in sick. I came in anytime I was asked, and I covered for all the other flakes in that office. The least my associate could do was give me a few sick days.

"I'll be fine. Lloyd, I'm afraid we won't get as much time

together as I typically prefer, but this is going to be a huge step forward for my future research. This will be more than enough money to ensure Bogdan and I can hit the ground running when he gets here in a few weeks."

All along, I'd been certain Kari Hobill was my golden goose, but every once in a while, fate had an ace up her sleeve.

25

Zane paced to the edge of the dry-erase board as he twirled a pen in his left hand. He and Sherry Cowen were the only two occupants of the incident room, as Amelia and Dean had left to speak to one of Kari Hobill's close friends. With the discovery of Kari's body the day before, the team had opted to keep working her case on a Saturday, and the faint scent of garlic still lingered from the pizza they'd ordered for lunch. He'd spent so much time in this room of late, even with the panoramic window looking out over nearby businesses and houses, Zane couldn't shake a sense of impending claustrophobia.

Oh well. I'll get over it.

He didn't have time to dwell on discomfort. Kari Hobill had been found twenty-four hours ago, and the clock was ticking for them to make a breakthrough. If they didn't get a lead from Kari, they'd no doubt be facing a seventh body soon.

Leveling the pen with the whiteboard, Zane turned to Sherry. "All right. One more time. What do they all have in common?"

"No kids. Great physical health. All except one lived in Cook County, and all six bodies were found south of Chicago. Only Kent Manning was married, but he was on the cusp of a divorce. None of the others had spouses. They all had steady, decent-paying jobs, but none were in the same industry. The only similarity is that they all had disposable income."

Sherry's recitation reminded Zane of a student preparing for their final exam.

He twirled the pen a few more times as he scanned the information scrawled across the whiteboard. "All had some form of post-high school education. Murphy Pendleton went to a trade school, and all the others attended colleges. Kari Hobill had an MSW, and Christine Fry had a master's. Maggie Hopkins and Kent Manning had bachelor's degrees, and Ollie Whitaker had an associate's. But none of them went to the same college, and none of them went to the same high school."

Sherry's chair creaked as she leaned back. "None of them even got their cars serviced in the same place. But there has to be something that connects them, right? Whether we're dealing with a professional who works for the Russian mob or a deranged serial killer, they have to find these people somewhere."

Resisting the urge to throw his hands up in the air, Zane pulled out a chair across from Sherry. "We've looked through their digital receipts to see if they even shopped in the same place before they were killed, but there was nothing."

Sherry rubbed her temple. "Then they're possibly linked by something they're keeping a secret, or somewhere they went a long time ago. How far back have we gone in their transaction history?"

"Six months." Zane had done plenty of the tedious research himself, and if a game show host popped up out of the floor to quiz him about the victims' routines before they died, he'd win a sizable chunk of money.

Sherry grew contemplative, but before they could sit in silence for long, the door swung open. Stepping over the threshold, Dean held the door as Amelia entered.

A nugget of hope emerged in Zane's thoughts, like a miner discovering the first signs of gold after he'd spent two weeks toiling in the depths of a cave. "Welcome back. How'd the chat with Hobill's friend go?"

Exchanging a glance with Dean, Amelia lifted a shoulder. "Not bad, but nothing groundbreaking."

Dean took a sip from his bottled water. "Hobill was good at her job, and all her coworkers liked her. Or at least none of them disliked her. She was a fan of running, exercising, and eating healthy. The friend said she'd lost almost forty pounds in the last few years, and she'd kept up the lifestyle ever since. That was a few years back, after she graduated with her master's."

Amelia took a seat next to Sherry. "Apparently, Kari bought her own treadmill, was hooked on the runner's high because she hated going to the gym. Her friend said she had some old stretch marks and excess skin from such rapid weight loss, and she always worried that people at the gym would be judgmental."

"Wait." Zane raised a hand as he racked his brain for the reason Amelia's statement seemed off. "Wait, didn't she buy a gym membership a few months ago? She didn't go a lot, but she did go."

"That's true." Leaning against the wall, Dean picked at the label of his water. "Her friend said she'd started going to a gym because she wanted to gain some muscle mass. And she'd gone to a plastic surgeon about the excess skin around her tummy. She'd had a tummy tuck, so she was a lot more confident."

For the second time, a light bulb buzzed to life in Zane's head. The imaginary game show host was holding out a microphone, watching intently as Zane struggled to come up with an answer.

"Why does plastic surgery sound so familiar?" Amelia echoed Zane's own thoughts. "Did one of the other victims see a cosmetic surgeon?"

As soon as Amelia finished her question, her head snapped up. Zane knew the puzzle pieces had clicked together for her as well.

Snapping his fingers, Zane shot Amelia a smile. "Yes, you're right. Kent Manning had surgery to remove a scar on his back. I talked to his friend, Royce Whitney, a few days after the interview with Tim Moreno. Royce said Kent had some kind of operation on his back when he was a kid, and it left a nasty scar. Kent's insurance wouldn't cover the removal, so he saved some money for a while. Because of the strain in Kent's marriage, he asked Royce to drive him to and from his surgery. At First Impressions."

Anticipation permeated the air like a living thing. Zane could tell the others were fighting the urge for a premature celebration, as this was easily the biggest lead they'd uncovered since the start of the case. Whether or not it would lead to a dead end, Zane couldn't say.

Amelia pulled out a small notebook and flipped through a few pages. "The name of the clinic Kari went to is First Impressions. Her friend also drove her to the appointment, then took her home."

Dean snatched up a dry-erase marker. "There's no way that's a coincidence."

Though Zane wasn't sure if the agent was stating a fact or trying to convince himself, his first inclination was to agree with Dean's assessment.

Hold off on jumping to any conclusions. Let's not count our ducks before they hatch, or however that saying goes.

Maybe two victims' affiliation with First Impressions was a coincidence, but to Zane, it was a promising coincidence. "Let's make some calls. Plastic surgery isn't exactly the type of thing people make announcements about, so if we want to find out whether the rest of the vics also went to First Impressions, we might have to dig a little."

Appearing thoughtful, Amelia set the notebook beside her laptop. "Well, in Kent and Kari's cases, they had close friends drive them to the clinic. Maybe that's where we ought to start with the others. Plastic surgery seems like something most people might confide in their best friends about, but probably not many others."

Dean scrawled *First Impressions* beneath Kent Manning and Kari Hobill's information on the whiteboard. "We've got four other victims to look through, so we can each take one. We can go back through the medical examiner's notes and see if he found anything during the postmortem. The M.E. might not have been able to tell if the vics had a scar removed or something like that, since the whole point of cosmetic surgery is to *remove* the scar. But if First Impressions is the common denominator between all our vics, it's possible someone else had a more noticeable procedure done."

As they each grabbed their phones and the files for their respective cases, all they were missing was a hearty *one, two, three, break!*

26

With all the information they'd compiled over the last week, Zane quickly located the contact information for Murphy's childhood best friend, Matthew Salazar. Salazar had been the person to report Pendleton missing, and the two had known one another since the second grade.

If any of Pendleton's friends would know about him going to a cosmetic surgeon, it's got to be Salazar, right?

Tapping Salazar's number into his phone, Zane slipped out into the hall. Two doors down, sunlight spilled through the open doorway of a smaller, unoccupied conference room. As he stepped inside, he initiated the call, pacing back and forth beside a circular table as the dial tone rang in his ear.

On the third ring, the line clicked to life. "Hello?"

"Afternoon, Mr. Salazar. This is Special Agent Palmer with the FBI. We spoke last week about your friend, Murphy Pendleton."

"Right, I remember." The man's tone was immediately more alert and responsive. "Can I help you with anything, Agent Palmer?"

"You can, actually. This might be a strange question, but do you know if Murphy had any cosmetic surgery? Not necessarily recent, but maybe sometime in the past few years?" Zane wanted to ensure he cast a wide net for this search. He didn't want to miss out on a common thread just because some time had passed.

"A...couple years ago, yeah. He had a work accident that messed up his foot, and I remember the doctor referred him to a plastic surgeon to help straighten out his toes or something."

Zane almost threw a victorious fist in the air, but he stopped himself. "And do you recall the name of the clinic he used?"

"Yeah, I think so. Hold on." Either Zane was projecting, or some of his determination had worn off on Salazar. "Wait, I've got it. First Impressions, that's the name of the place where Murphy went. He felt weird going to a plastic surgeon's office, but the receptionist told him they got referrals from other doctors all the time. I remember that because I was there when he went in for his consultation. He couldn't drive because his foot was still messed up and he had a manual transmission."

Salazar's explanation was like music to Zane's ears. After thanking the man for his time, Zane all but sprinted back to the incident room.

As much as he wanted to burst in with his announcement, he tempered his excitement. Sherry was alone at the table, her phone pressed to her ear with her shoulder as she typed a few quick words on her laptop. "All right. No, that's okay. You've been very helpful. Just give me a call if you think of anything else, no matter what time of day. Okay. Take care. Bye."

Cocking an eyebrow for a silent question, Zane circled around the table to the whiteboard. "No luck?"

Sherry shook her head as she crossed out the first line on her notepad. "No, but that was just the first call. Maggie Hopkins didn't have a ton of close friends, but she has two sisters, one of whom lives in Chicago. The friend I just spoke with suggested I give that sister a call, so that's my next stop." Her curious gaze shifted to him. "What about you?"

With a grin, Zane scrawled *First Impressions* at the bottom of the Murphy Pendleton section of the whiteboard. "Pendleton's friend, Matthew Salazar, took him to his consultation at First Impressions. Pendleton was referred there after a work accident."

Sherry rubbed her hands together. "It's possible that two were a coincidence. Somewhat unlikely, but still possible. But three? No way. That can't be a coincidence."

"I'm going to start looking into this clinic while you guys work on following up with the rest of the vics." Zane dropped down to his seat and powered on his laptop. After a week of what had been mostly tedium, their team had shifted into gear and was operating like a well-oiled machine.

While Sherry phoned Maggie's sister, Zane pulled up the website of First Impressions. Fortunately for him, the clinic dedicated a section of the site to the surgeons, nurses, and others who worked at the clinic. From the receptionist to the owner, Roger McKay, each employee's name, bio, and photo was included. For the handful of surgeons, the site also added credentials and their areas of expertise.

Before Zane had even started to research the surgeons of First Impressions, Sherry wrapped up her call. "Maggie's sister confirmed she went to First Impressions for a breast reduction. The procedure took place a little over a year before Maggie disappeared."

We sure as hell aren't dealing with a coincidence now.

With Zane and Sherry's respective tasks complete, they split up the personnel from First Impressions and got to work. This was usually the time of day when Zane required a cup of coffee to tide him over to the end of his shift, but today, he was fueled by a sense of direction and purpose.

All the while, Zane's hopes remained balanced on a wire.

What if neither of the other victims was affiliated with First Impressions? Where would that leave them?

No, he couldn't think about that right now. The search into the backgrounds of the staff at First Impressions required his full focus.

Less than halfway through the list of names, Amelia returned. She didn't even have to speak for Zane to realize she'd connected Christine Fry to First Impressions—he could read it in her focused expression. Dean entered the room shortly afterward, but Zane was less adept at discerning his body language.

Without offering a greeting to the three of them, Dean snatched the dry-erase marker and scrawled the name of the clinic beneath Ollie Whitaker's portion of the whiteboard.

Amelia glanced up from her laptop. "That's all six of them, then. No wonder we didn't find the connection in the background research we did. Maggie Hopkins had her procedure done more than a year before she went missing, and Murphy Pendleton's occurred almost two years before he disappeared. And none of them were procedures many would notice unless they were close to the victims."

Pulling out a chair, Dean swept his gaze over the little group. "You've all been looking into this clinic, right? What've you got so far?"

Zane turned his laptop around for Dean to see. "Not a lot, but I don't think any of us expected a neon sign declaring who may or may not be affiliated with organ trafficking. The business itself is clean. They pay their taxes, renew their permits when they need to, and comply with all the city and state regulations for their industry."

Dean scanned the screen. "Fair enough. What about the staff?"

"Not much there either." Sherry gestured to her computer. "I ran background checks on the two senior surgeons, and they're just as clean as the clinic. Just two normal people who happen to be really good at what they do."

The rundown didn't seem promising, but Zane refused to let go of his sense of hope. "The other two surgeons seem typical too. Clean criminal records, good grades in med school. One is married with a kid in college and another in high school, and the other is married with three step-kids."

Dean placed his chin in his palm. "How about nurses? Anesthesiologists?"

Sherry shook her head. "There are only two nurses and two anesthesiologists, and so far, nothing about them is jumping out. We can do more thorough research on them, though. And at this point, it might be a good idea for us to go talk to the owner of the clinic. He'll know more about his staff than we do, and honestly, he could be a person of interest. It'd be good to get a read on him."

"Good idea." Zane made a quick call to First Impressions and learned Roger McKay was working from home that day. He snatched up his car keys and shot Sherry an expectant look. "We can head to McKay's place to see if we can catch him at home."

Dean pushed away Zane's laptop and reached for his own. "All right. We'll get started on that deep dive review of the First Impressions staff."

Amelia offered Dean and Zane a thumps-up, a gesture he suspected she'd picked up from Sherry. "Sounds good. We'll keep you posted if we find anything."

With a quick salute, Zane pulled open the door. "We'll do the same."

For the first time in well over a week, Zane could make out a clear path forward in the investigation.

27

For close to twenty minutes, Amelia and Dean worked in silence. From where they were tucked away in the incident room on the field office's fifth floor, the only sounds other than the building's ventilation were the clicks of their keyboards. Not that Amelia minded—they'd entered crunch time, and the clock was their enemy. Each second that passed was another moment when the killer could set his sights on a new victim or, God forbid, kill someone he'd already kidnapped.

She and Dean had started their in-depth research on the staff trained in surgical procedure, since the perp who'd killed their six victims was most assuredly a surgeon. Neither of them had ruled out the rest of the employees at First Impressions, but surgeons were the most logical starting point.

What exactly were they searching for? Amelia still wasn't one hundred percent sure. Any abnormality to indicate one of the staff was involved in a shady side business, she figured. If any of them had landed themselves on the Bureau's dark web-related watchlists in the past, if they'd been sued for egregious malpractice, or if their lifestyle was too ritzy for their reported income.

She was glad Sherry and Zane had gone to interview Roger McKay. Even with a clear common thread between their victims, matching up the how and why was still a feat in and of itself.

There was always the possibility the killer didn't work for First Impressions. In the twenty-first century, the perp could have found a way to hack the clinic's databases to access patient records. If they were indeed dealing with a cartel or the Russians, hacking would fit cleanly into their modi operandi.

Amelia shook off the doubts. She'd already made Layton Redker aware of the newest development, and he'd assured her he was on his way to Cyber Crimes to inform them. If First Impressions had experienced a data breach, Cyber would find it.

As Amelia typed in the first and last name of the third surgeon on their list, her cell buzzed against the table. In her periphery, Dean jolted upright in his chair. Offering Dean an apologetic glance, she scooped up the phone. "Sorry about that. I don't recognize the number, but it's a Chicago area code." She took the call. "Agent Storm speaking."

"Good afternoon, Agent. I'm Deputy Lynda Christensen with the Cook County Sheriff's Department." The woman rattled off her credentials, assuring Amelia she was indeed who she claimed to be. All the while, Amelia's curiosity rose like floodwaters.

"Afternoon, Deputy. How can I help you?"

"Well, I'm handling our tip line right now, and I've got a caller on the line who says he has information about a woman who went missing from Shady Oak a couple weeks ago, Kari Hobill. I understand from the young woman's father that you're the agent on her case."

Amelia's spine straightened of its own volition, her senses keen. "I'm one of the agents, yes."

"Oh, good. The caller has already given his information to me, along with the gist of what he was calling about. I'll transfer him over to you, if that's okay. And I can give you his number in case the call gets dropped."

"Of course. I can take it down now."

As the deputy read out the name and number, Amelia scribbled the information in her notebook. With excitement humming beneath her skin, she thanked Deputy Christensen and waited for the transfer to go through. All the while, Dean glanced at her, back to his laptop, then back at her.

"Witness," Amelia mouthed as the line clicked over.

Dean's eyebrows shot up his forehead, but he remained quiet.

"Um, hello? Is this…the FBI?" The male on the other end of the line was young, and his voice radiated nervousness.

Amelia swiveled her chair to face the window. "Hello, you must be Mitch? I'm Special Agent Storm with the FBI."

"Okay, hi. Yeah, I'm Mitch Raymond. I'm…sorry I called the wrong place. I saw that lady, Kari, on the news channel's website a little bit ago. The article was from earlier in the week, but I just called the number I saw there."

"That's all right, there's nothing to be sorry about. I understand you had a tip you were calling in?"

"Right, yeah." Some of his anxiety dissipated, his tone now more purposeful. "I saw her. Kari Hobill. I was at Casey Park taking pictures of some plants for my science class, and I ran into her when I was coming up from the banks of the creek that runs through it."

Rather than write in her notebook, Amelia opened a text document on her laptop, switched the call to speaker, and typed out an abbreviated account of Mitch's statement. "Did you talk to her at all?"

"Sort of. She asked me what I was doing down by the creek, so I told her about the assignment I'm doing for my class. I think she thought it was weird, because it was still pretty early in spring and most of the plants were dead, but I told her that was part of what the assignment was about."

"Did you notice anything strange about her demeanor? Was she looking over her shoulder, or did she seem scared, anything like that?"

"No, I don't think so. She was cautious with me, some guy hanging out by the creek, but I couldn't really blame her. After I told her about the class assignment, I headed back to the parking lot while she kept going on the walking trail. My mom was picking me up, so I decided to take some pictures up around the parking lot."

"Do you know if anyone was with Kari at the park?"

"No, she seemed alone. But...there was this dude just sitting in his car with all his windows rolled up. The car wasn't on, but he was just sitting there. It was really weird, you know? It was one of those things that just gives you the creeps, and you don't really know why. I tried to ignore him, and I took a few more pictures before my mom got there to pick me up. She saw him, too, if you want to talk to her."

Amelia's palms went clammy, anticipation building in her stomach as Mitch finished his account. "Do either of you remember any details about this man or his car? A license plate, maybe, or his general appearance?" Amelia wondered if it was too much to hope the boy's photos included one of the car.

"Um...yeah, I think so."

"Just describe what you remember to me."

"Okay. The car was silver, and it was a Toyota. A Camry, I think? But maybe a Corolla. Four doors. The guy in the driver's seat looked like he was kinda old, like the same age as my dad, so probably about fifty?"

Fifty is old now?

Amelia chuckled to herself. Kids always thought their parents were ancient. She kept the thought to herself as she typed out Mitch's description. "Did you notice anything specific about his appearance? A tattoo or a scar, maybe?"

"No." The poor kid's tone went from determined and helpful to flat-out discouraged in record time. "But I did get a picture. Not of him, but I got the license plate of his car in one of the plant pictures I took. I cropped it out for my assignment, but I still have the original. Can I send it to you?" *Oh thank God.*

"Absolutely." Amelia gave him her work email and waited impatiently until the message popped up in her inbox.

As she opened the file, she expected the plate number to be partially obscured or blurry, as roadblocks had become the norm in this investigation. She was pleasantly surprised to find a high-definition photo of a brown, brittle-looking shrub and a crystal-clear license plate behind it.

After thanking Mitch for the information and setting up a time later in the evening for his mother to bring him to the field office to provide an official statement, Amelia set down her phone and zoomed in on the plate. She scooted closer to Dean and turned the laptop for him to see.

Dean's eyes widened. "A license plate? And we think that's our guy?"

"He might not be, but he was there with Kari in the same location, and at the same time, she was last seen. We've got Mitch Raymond and his mother coming in for an official statement, so we'll have everything on record."

Rubbing his chin, Dean leaned back in his chair. "This might sound outlandish, but what about the possibility Mitch or his mom had something to do with Kari disappearing? They were also in the same location where it's presumed she disappeared, considering her car was found there a few days after she went missing."

"No, I don't think so. We'll keep our eyes and ears open when the Raymonds come in to give their statement, but Mitch is just a kid. We can check the DMV, but he might not even have his driver's license. He's definitely not the perp who cut out the vics' organs, and my gut tells me he's genuinely trying to be helpful right now."

"Yeah, I think you're right." Dean gestured to Amelia's laptop. "Let's take a look at this plate and see where it takes us."

Considering all the time Amelia had spent dealing with organized criminal empires—mafiosos were well versed in swapping out license plates to throw off the authorities in the event their vehicles were spotted in the commission of a crime—she was about seventy percent sure the Toyota would lead them nowhere. The sentiment might have been pessimistic, but with all the new leads they'd uncovered today, she strove to keep her expectations grounded in reality.

As she entered the license plate into the database, excitement stirred in the air when a result populated the screen.

Dean propped his arms on the table and leaned in closer to the computer. "The plate's registered to Louis James Sherman. That name is familiar."

Amelia highlighted the text displaying the make and model of the vehicle. "And it's the right license plate. Silver Toyota Corolla sedan, purchased two years ago by Louis James Sherman from a dealership here in Chicago. Let's take a look at Mr. Sherman."

A light tremor had made its way to Amelia's hands as she punched in Sherman's information. It was the moment of truth—the moment they'd learn if Louis James Sherman fit the bill for the perp they sought.

Less than halfway down the page, Amelia got her answer.

Blinking a few times, as if she expected the result to change, she turned to Dean. "There's a Lou Sherman who works at First Impressions. That's why his name sounded familiar. We must've seen it on their website."

Dean flipped back over to the First Impressions website tab he had open on his laptop. "He's an assistant? Says on your screen that he's got an MD. Why is he an assistant when he has a medical degree?"

Amelia made a show of stretching her fingers. "Let's find out. All right, so First Impressions is his current employer, and before that...he worked for a hospital. As a surgeon." She clicked a link and typed in a few more search terms. "He was fired from the hospital three years ago after he received his second malpractice suit."

Dean squinted at the screen. "A lot of those terms are complete jargon to me, but he was sued for malpractice for performing a risky surgery when the patient didn't actually need surgery? Is that the gist of it? And the patient was paralyzed from the waist down as a result?"

"Yeah, that's right. Lost his medical license too." As much as Amelia wished she could leap out of her chair and head straight to Lou Sherman's condo, she kept her ass planted and grabbed her cell, pulling up Cassandra Halcott's name. "Let me get ahold of the assistant U.S. attorney. This is all circumstantial evidence, but there's enough of it for a search warrant at the very least. If we're going to pick up Lou Sherman for an interview, I want to make sure we can surprise him with a warrant, so he doesn't have time to destroy any evidence."

"All right. I'll shoot a message to Cowen, so she and Palmer know about it."

Amelia and the team's next move had to be decisive and swift. They weren't certain if the suspect was acting alone, if he was affiliated with a cartel, or if he and a few of his cohorts had started up a new organ-trafficking business separate from the criminal organizations in Cook County.

Whatever his role, Amelia's instincts screamed that Lou Sherman was involved.

Question was, had he acted alone, or were they up against an entire team?

—————

28

S unlight spilling in through the living room picture
window had turned a darker shade of gold, serving as a
reminder to Amelia that time was slipping through their
fingers. To her dismay, Lou Sherman had been nowhere in
sight when they'd arrived at his seventh-story condo. The
property was close to the FBI office, so at least she'd been
spared an agonizing drive across town.

Along with Amelia and Dean, two crime scene techs,
Trisha Pruitt and Norman Odgers, had accompanied them to
the residence.

Sherman's place was modestly decorated, sparse, sterile.
Truth be told, Amelia could have easily convinced herself she
was sitting in a dentist's office.

Movement from a short hall next to the dining area drew
Amelia's attention as Dean made his way to the living room.
"Nothing promising in the bedroom or bathroom. Odgers is
heading to the second bedroom now. Just wanted to see if
you guys found anything out here."

Amelia gestured to the short, curly haired woman near
the table. "Pruitt is about to look through the bookshelf

while I get started on the living room. There was nothing in the dining room except a cactus and a bookshelf full of classic novels."

Peering around the sunlit space, Dean seemed like he was about to make an observation.

Before the words could leave his lips, Trisha Pruitt threw one hand in the air. "I think I might've found something."

Curiosity shot through Amelia like an electrical charge. Exchanging a vehement glance with Dean, the two of them started for the dining room. "What is it?"

"This book. There's paper shoved in between the pages." Pruitt set a hardcover copy of *Huckleberry Finn* on the dining table. As Amelia and Dean approached, she flipped open the book and pulled out a folded sheet of paper. "There's also a laptop charger under the table by the cactus, but I haven't seen a computer anywhere."

Dean gestured toward the hall. "We didn't see anything back in the bedroom either. The only electronics I've noticed so far are the television and the cable box in the living room. From the looks of it, the second bedroom was just used for storage, so I doubt we'll find Sherman's laptop in there."

Amelia heaved a mental sigh. More than likely, Lou Sherman's laptop was with him.

Wherever the hell that is.

"Well, this might help us find something." Pruitt unfolded the slip of paper, smoothing it before she slid it across the table to Amelia and Dean. "It's an electric bill for this month, but it's not for this address. Not for Lou Sherman either. It's for some company called Enduring Resilience."

Dean's eyebrows knitted together as he peered down at the document. "That's one hell of an electric bill. I haven't done a lot of work on drug busts, but Sherry used to. This is about on par with the expenses you'd expect to see from an illegal grow house back in the day."

"Let me see what this place looks like." Amelia retrieved her phone and entered the address into a mapping app. "Looks like this place is about an hour's drive from where we are now, at least in current traffic. It's just south of the city."

"All the bodies were found in rural areas south of Chicago." Dean tapped a gloved finger next to the address.

Amelia switched from the map to a web browser. She wished she had a proper computer to run all the information through federal databases, but she'd have to do her best with the resources available. "Enduring Resilience...turned up a bunch of nothing. Just search results for dictionary definitions and articles about what resilience is. One second, let me try adding *Chicago* or *Illinois* at the end of it."

As Amelia inputted a handful of terms into the search engine, Pruitt leafed through a few pages in *The Grapes of Wrath* and produced another folded sheet of paper. Pausing in her online pursuit for information about Enduring Resilience, Amelia peeked at the newest document.

"Wait a second." She looked at Dean and then Pruitt. "This is an invoice?"

Dean whistled through his teeth. "And it ain't a cheap one. One hundred and fifty thousand for an...extracorporeal membrane oxygenation machine. ECMO for short."

Though the terminology was familiar to Amelia, she couldn't say she knew any specifics about the technology.

Fortunately for her and Dean, Trisha Pruitt jumped in to save them from another internet search. "My brother's a doctor in Iowa. His hospital uses ECMO machines. The first time he mentioned ECMO, I asked him all kinds of questions." She lifted a shoulder. "Curious by nature, so I guess that's why I'm a crime scene analyst. But anyway, they bypass the need to have functioning lungs and even a functioning heart."

"A heart and lung machine." For the second time in the

investigation, Amelia's medical knowledge came from her consumption of medical dramas.

Pruitt nodded. "Exactly. Only with ECMO, the patient can be awake and actually function. The doctors insert tubes into major arteries and veins, like the femoral artery, and then the machine oxygenates the blood and pumps it back through the body. It's the big guns of life support, but there have been exceptional cases where people spent a few weeks on ECMO and ultimately recovered."

Dean drummed his fingers against the invoice. "This was billed to that same business, Enduring Resilience. I'm going to send that name over to Redker and see if they can dig up anything on it back at the office. It smells like a shell company to me."

Amelia's excitement transformed into professional determination. "Let me send a quick message to Dr. Francis and see what he knows about ECMO. I'm sure he's got a lot more knowledge about that system than any of us. He might even be able to tell us if he thinks ECMO was used on the victims before they were killed."

In Amelia's head, she pictured a cold, sterile room with a bedridden Kari Hobill hooked up to various catheters and tubes that circulated her blood to keep her barely alive. The imagery sent goose bumps down her spine, but realizing the horror all six victims had endured also flared her ire.

"We need to get all this over to the assistant U.S. attorney." Dean rapped his knuckles on the table beside the invoice. "Along with whatever else is in that book. My guess is that Sherman thought he had a clever hiding place by tucking all these documents in plain sight inside these classics."

Trisha Pruitt flipped through Anne Frank's *The Diary of a Young Girl* and retrieved another sheet of paper. "As far as hiding spots go, it's certainly not the worst I've seen.

Honestly, it's more clever than a false bottom in a drawer, if you ask me. False bottoms are easier to locate, and almost every crime scene tech is going to be on the lookout for them. But hiding important paperwork in a copy of *Huckleberry Finn*? I can see someone missing that in a search."

Good thing we didn't.

As Amelia tapped out a quick text message to the forensic pathologist, she glanced at Dean. "I think we might have enough right here for a warrant for that property, and enough to subpoena any business records affiliated with Enduring Resilience."

Pruitt jumped in. "But if you want to make sure, wait for Dr. Francis to go through his postmortem exam notes and see if ECMO is consistent with the victims' injuries."

"Measure twice, cut once. Same concept here, is that what you're saying?" Dean arched a brow. "Problem with that is if Sherman isn't here, then he's somewhere else, doing only God-knows-what. If he's our guy, which it's starting to seem pretty dang likely that he is—"

"He's off playing operation on another vic as we speak." Amelia couldn't have agreed more.

With every passing second, they risked Lou Sherman disappearing, or worse. At the absolute least, the man was a viable lead, and at the worst...well.

Sherman had answers, and they needed to find him.

29

As Zane sipped from his mug of hot coffee, he glanced out the tall window as a car slowed almost to a complete stop before lumbering over a speed bump in front of the McKay residence. Mentally, Zane cringed as he recalled how he'd slammed on the brakes upon noticing the miniature mountain at the last second. Though the McKay family's house was in a more upscale section of the city, Roger McKay's wife, Dawn, had told Zane and Sherry about past issues with cars zipping through the neighborhood at twenty over the speed limit. The solution? A speed bump the size of Mount Olympus.

The agents were admitted to the McKay house and offered snacks, which they politely declined. As for the interview? That was a different story.

Brushing off the front of her dark wash jeans, Dawn McKay pushed herself off the club chair. "That's Roger's car. I'm sorry you had to wait so long."

Sherry offered Dawn a reassuring smile. "It's all right. Thank you again for the coffee and the cookies. That was very nice of you."

Dawn's eyes brightened, and the faint hum of the garage door on the other side of the house drifted through the living area. With the reclaimed wood of the coffee table and matching end tables, as well as the black-and-red checked blanket resting along the back of the sectional couch, the rustic decor could have almost tricked Zane into believing he was at a cabin instead of a house in the middle of one of the country's biggest cities.

For the past forty-five minutes, he and Sherry had been treated as if they were Dr. Dawn McKay's guests. According to Dawn, a physics professor at the University of Illinois Chicago, her and her husband's busy schedules rarely allowed them to invite friends or family over. Even though Zane and Sherry were FBI agents, Dawn insisted they make themselves comfortable while waiting for her husband to return home from a work-related meeting. He'd stepped out after wrapping up the business he could complete at home.

To say Dawn McKay was nice would have been an understatement. If Roger McKay turned out to be a jerk—and especially if Roger was involved in an organ-trafficking business—Zane had reached the point where he'd be personally offended on Dawn's behalf. He'd kept an open mind regarding the potential for Dawn's involvement, but the likelihood grew slimmer with every word she spoke.

Zane shook off the thoughts as the motor of the garage door stopped. Glancing at Sherry, he rose to stand.

As he waited in silence for Dawn to usher Roger into the living room, a litany of what-if scenarios whipped through Zane's head. On the nearly one-hour drive to the McKay residence, Sherry had discovered that Roger McKay and Lou Sherman had attended medical school together. The pair had gone their separate ways after graduation, with Lou heading into emergency medicine and Roger specializing in reconstructive surgery.

Had Roger hired Lou Sherman so they could begin an organ-trafficking operation while using First Impressions as cover? Had Sherman simply used his position at the clinic to seek out victims for his own trafficking business? Considering the brief review Sherry had conducted of the clinic's finances, there were no discrepancies to indicate the clinic raked in any sort of illegal profit. Maybe Sherman used the long-standing friendship to blind McKay to his depravity.

We don't typically suspect those closest to us of being capable of such heinous acts.

Joseph Larson flashed in Zane's mind. He'd hope it was that, as Dawn McKay appeared to be the opposite of a criminal.

The unfortunate truth of the matter was that Zane still had far more questions than answers. He could speculate on Roger McKay's involvement in organ trafficking until he was blue in the face, but hypotheticals would get him nowhere.

Muffled voices drew Zane's attention to the arched doorway leading to the foyer. With one hand on her husband's shoulder, Dawn McKay led Roger into the living room, the warm smile still on her face. "Honey, these are Special Agents Palmer," she pointed to Zane, "and Cowen. They tried to call you before stopping by, but you were in that meeting. I knew you'd want to talk to them, so I asked them to wait."

A hint of nervousness flickered in Roger's expression, but it was no more intense than what Zane would expect from an average person dealing with the FBI.

"All right. Sorry you had to wait. We're looking to expand my clinic to a second location, and the only meeting I could get with the real estate company was on a Saturday, if you can believe that."

Zane shot him a grin. "I can. Weekend meetings are surprisingly common at the Bureau too."

Squeezing Roger's shoulder, Dawn returned Zane's smile. "I'll let you have the room to yourselves. I've got some assignments I need to start grading. Finals seem like they're right around the corner."

Physics had never been Zane's strong suit, and he couldn't quell a pang of sympathy for those brave enough to soldier through a college-level physics course. How anyone pulled off a doctorate in the field, he'd never know.

Clearing her throat, Sherry motioned toward the club chair where Dawn had been seated. "As I'm sure you suspected, we have some questions we'd like to ask you."

Roger made his way to the chair. "Of course. Honestly, I'm in the dark as to what the FBI might want to ask me. What can I help you with?"

As best as Zane could tell, the man's confusion was genuine. His posture was a bit stiff, but nothing about his demeanor hinted at defensiveness. "We'd like to know more about one of the men who works at your clinic. Lou Sherman."

Roger took his seat, his shoulders slumping like they'd just been saddled with a barbell. "Lou Sherman? Yeah, I hired him for my clinic a couple years ago."

Zane dropped to sit, followed by Sherry. Elbows propped on her legs, Sherry fixed her gaze on Roger. "We understand Mr. Sherman also has a medical degree, but his license to practice was revoked after he received two malpractice suits in the span of six months, one of which left a patient paralyzed from the waist down."

Heaving a sigh, Roger rubbed his eyes. "I'm aware. And I'm sure you're aware that Lou and I attended medical school together. If you're wondering why I hired him, well...there are a lot of nuances to malpractice suits. Sometimes, the people filing them can be grieving, or they can be upset because of a specific medical outcome they weren't expecting. It doesn't mean the physician was incompetent or acting with malice, you know? More often than not, it means they made a mistake. Human error. Or the operation was high-risk."

"You said you hired Lou a couple years ago." Zane retrieved a pen and a small notebook from his suit pocket.

"Right." Roger folded his hands in his lap. "I assume that's why he sought me out when he was looking for work. He said he wanted to find a position in the medical field, and at the time, I had an opening. I remembered Lou being a smart guy, and he was always organized. I felt a little bad since he'd lost his medical license, and I know how hard it can be finding a job in this field with that black mark on your record. Plus, it's not like he'd be making any medical decisions for our patients."

To get an unbiased account of Lou's history at First Impressions, neither Zane nor Sherry had mentioned Lou's potential involvement in six open murder cases. Plus, if Roger was involved in the organ-trafficking ring, they could use the same tactic to get him to slip up and reveal more than they'd asked for.

With the basics out of the way, Zane decided it was time to dig a little deeper. "Have you been following the news, Dr. McKay?"

Roger shook his head. "No. I know, it makes me sound like I'm willfully ignorant, but to be honest? The news just brings me down. Dawn keeps up with it, and she tells me some of the stories, but that's about it."

Well, that might explain why McKay hadn't noticed that six of his former patients had been murdered. "We're here today because we're investigating six related homicides, and all the victims were patients at First Impressions."

The color drained from Roger's face. "I'm...sorry, murders? My patients? Are you sure?"

Sherry rattled off the victims' names, and Roger went from shocked to borderline despondent.

"Their names are familiar, but I'll admit I don't remember them all. I have three other surgeons who work with me. We usually take referrals for reconstructive surgeries, but we also do cosmetic procedures, though they aren't the bulk of our clients. I do recall Kari and Murphy. They were both great people, and I'm heartbroken that something so awful happened to them." Rolling his shoulders, Roger straightened, determination overtaking his sadness. "All right. Whatever help I can give, I'm happy to provide."

Zane's doubts about Roger's involvement in organ trafficking deepened. Either the man had missed his calling as an Academy Award-winning actor, or he was telling the truth.

Technically, every employee at First Impressions was a person of interest. However, based on the invoices and utility bills found hidden at Lou Sherman's residence, as well as the presence of his car at Kari's last known location, Lou Sherman was at the top of the list. And considering Amelia and Dean hadn't been able to find the man, they were dealing with the very real possibility that Sherman might've split town and disappeared.

Sherry reached for her mug. "What more can you tell us about Lou Sherman? Has he been behaving differently lately?"

"He called me yesterday to tell me he wasn't feeling well, and he needed a couple days off work. I didn't question it much, since his attendance is usually stellar. He did take some personal time the other week too. Said he was working on a side project he'd put together to make some extra cash."

That's one way to put it.

"Are you always open on the weekend?"

He nodded. "Yes. Since most people work during the week, we've found having weekend hours very profitable."

As Zane jotted down his notes, Sherry posed the next question. "I know it's been a while since Kari Hobill and the others had their procedures done, but do you ever recall Sherman taking a special interest in any of the patients at the clinic?"

Lips pursed, Roger scratched his chin, deep in thought. "Now that you mention it, I do recall him seeming especially interested in Kari Hobill's outcome. Murphy's too. Lou isn't the sentimental type, but I remember him asking me about their follow-up appointments. At the time, I thought it was just lingering medical curiosity."

With each additional question Zane and Sherry posed to Roger, Zane grew more and more confident Lou Sherman was involved in the kidnapping and murder of the six victims.

What they couldn't determine was if the man had an accomplice or whether he'd been hired by a cartel. Were they dealing with a single psychotic surgeon or a Mexican drug cartel? Or the Russian mob?

By the time Zane and Sherry finished the interview with Roger, they were no closer to answering that million-dollar question.

30

A melia peered at the darkening horizon in the rearview mirror, wishing they'd been able to get the warrant for Lou Sherman's so-called business property when it was still light outside. Between her, Dean, and the tactical team, they had enough flashlights to illuminate the entire planet, but Amelia was pointedly aware of how much more difficult it was to spot booby traps in the dark.

Memories of another nighttime raid hovered on the edges of Amelia's thoughts. Several months ago, in a different part of rural Illinois, a similar night had ended in a surprise explosion that claimed the lives of three sheriff's deputies. With the acrid scent of smoke still fresh in her mind, Amelia was determined that tonight would end differently than the takedown of the Fox Creek Butcher.

The team's frustration over the circumstances around this raid was amplified when their request to have a medical team on-site had been denied. She could only hope that short-sighted view wouldn't add another victim to the tally.

As the trees beside the road thinned and a single-story ranch-style home appeared, Amelia shook off the recollection. With the FBI's highly trained tactical team accompanying her and Dean, as well as a second wave of backup not far behind them, she was in good hands. The Bureau taught its raid teams how to spot traps and improvised explosives, and they had access to state-of-the-art technology to monitor their surroundings.

From the driver's seat, Tom Harris, one of the lead tactical agents at the Chicago Field Office, gestured toward the house as he clicked off the headlights. "I only see one vehicle parked in the driveway."

Amelia leaned forward, poking her head around the passenger's seat. "It's a silver Toyota Corolla, same make and model as Sherman's car. I can't quite see the plates from here, but more than likely, it's his car."

To Amelia's side, Dean adjusted the Kevlar vest he wore beneath a navy-blue FBI jacket. "He could still have people with him. More perps and victims."

"As soon as I put our signal jammer online, anyone in that house won't be able to reach out for backup, and it'll knock out any security cameras around the place. Which in and of itself is a warning, but at least they won't have eyes on us." The woman in the passenger seat was Emily Wilson, another tenured agent from the tactical team. Having her and Tom Harris accompanying them to serve the warrant kept a portion of Amelia's concerns at bay.

A drop of sweat beaded between Amelia's shoulder blades, and she couldn't wait to get out of the SUV and step into the cool night air. "While the assistant U.S. attorney was getting the warrant for this place, we consulted with some of my colleagues in Organized Crime. They specialize in the Mexican drug cartels, and they hadn't heard of either cartel operating in organ trafficking around Chicago."

Dean nodded. "We couldn't find any affiliation between Sherman and the Russians either. Doesn't mean it isn't there, but it's safe to say he isn't any kind of major player in the Russian mob or the drug cartels."

"Well, that's reassuring." Tom Harris chuckled, and for the life of her, Amelia couldn't tell if the man was being sarcastic.

Amelia and Zane had done their best to track down any links between Lou Sherman and any criminal organization, but they'd come up with nothing. Back at the FBI office, Layton Redker had stayed behind to help Cyber Crimes as they worked to uncover dark web activity that might have been perpetrated by Sherman. According to Layton, the search was like trying to find a needle in a mountain of hay, but they'd be remiss if they didn't give it a shot.

The goal of their efforts was simple—Amelia and the others wanted to know if they were about to waltz into a den of mafiosos or if Lou Sherman was acting alone. There was still the possibility, albeit slim, that Lou Sherman wasn't involved at all, but a judge had decided they'd collected enough evidence for a thorough warrant.

As the SUV pulled to a stop along the edge of the front yard, Amelia adjusted the straps of her vest and double-checked her service weapon. Meanwhile, Dean tucked the paper copy of their warrant into the front of his vest.

Harris glanced at the rearview mirror. "All right. Let's meet up with the rest of the team and figure out our places." His tone was so calm and collected, he could've been placing an order at a deli counter.

Shoving open her door, Amelia hopped out onto the soft grass. Her hopes for a cool, refreshing breeze were quickly dashed. Humidity had permeated the air since they'd left the field office, leaving the world around them damp and heavy. The earthy scent of woodland detritus wafted over to them along the sprawling yard. Were they in any other situation, Amelia could have found the scene peaceful.

But not tonight. Not with the potential for a madman's traps on the horizon.

From a second SUV, four more agents clad in full tactical gear emerged. With an upraised hand, Tom Harris beckoned them over. "Richmond and Walsh, I've jammed any signals, so I want the two of you to scout the perimeter, working your way toward the house. Make it thorough but quick, and report back here as soon as you're finished."

The taller of the pair pulled down his night vision goggles. "Yes, sir." Motioning to his counterpart, the pair took off toward the house.

On the drive to Lou Sherman's rural property, Tom had explained the roles of his team. Richmond and Walsh both had experience in not only diffusing explosives, but in locating them as well.

Without knowing exactly what they were up against, he was taking no chances.

Harris gestured to the other two agents. "Rosario, Preston, you'll go with Walsh and Richmond to the back of the house. Wilson and I will take the front along with Agents Storm and Steelman. Our backup ought to be here within the next ten, but you know what they say about too many cooks in the kitchen. If we need them, we'll radio 'em in. Otherwise, they're going to monitor the exterior."

Though Amelia wasn't sure how long the pair of explosives experts needed to sweep the exterior of the house, she braced herself for the same kind of wait she'd expect at the dentist's office. She tried to busy herself by adjusting her earpiece until it fit just right—radio signals weren't blocked by their jammer—but the endeavor still gave her mind plenty of room to wander. Whenever uncertainty loomed ahead of her, she preferred to dive straight in so she could get answers to her questions.

Each passing second thickened the tension in the air, and Amelia was certain the sensation wasn't just the humidity.

She hated the waiting game.

What was in that damn house? Sherman was here, wasn't he? There was only one vehicle registered in his name, and it sat in the driveway. Though Amelia didn't spot the glow of a light through any of the windows, Sherman could easily be in an interior room, or he could have blackout curtains. With the hint of lingering daylight on the horizon, they weren't yet surrounded by pitch blackness, so the muted glow of a light through curtains was still difficult to see.

Had Sherman disappeared through a secret exit? Just because there was nothing like that on the county's blueprint for the place didn't mean anything. Lou wouldn't be the first suspect to make his own additions to a property without seeking legal approval.

If he bolted, he's going to be on foot. He won't get far. We'll find him.

In the low light, Richmond and Walsh were little more than shadows as they trotted toward the parked SUVs.

"Perimeter is clear." Richmond, who stood a couple inches taller than Amelia's five-eight frame, waved a hand at the house. "We saw a light on around back. Looked like it might've been in a kitchen or something. Didn't spot any movement, though."

The light was a good sign.

So is the lack of booby traps.

Amelia swallowed a mirthless chortle. "All right. Let's serve this warrant."

Tom Harris unshouldered a portable battering ram. "Lead the way. We're right behind you."

Nerves bristled beneath Amelia's skin as she and Dean started for the covered porch. Despite the reassurance of knowing two tactical experts had swept the area, she still braced herself for a deafening blast or the sudden order to get down as gunfire rained down on them.

For a beat, the scents of sand and dust took the place of grass and earth, and her mind's eye brought her back to a small desert compound about the same size as the ranch.

Amelia gave herself a mental slap.

This isn't the Middle East. This is northern Illinois, less than an hour south of Chicago.

As they neared the stairs, she took in a lungful of the humid night air. No dust, no acrid stench of gunpowder. Just the fresh scent of spring.

Pulling the warrant from his vest, Dean raised a hand to pound on the door. Each knock cut through the air with the force of a gunshot, reminding Amelia just how still the world was outside the city.

"This is the Federal Bureau of Investigation, and we have a warrant. Open the door, or we will break it down." Dean jiggled the handle, but it was locked.

"No activity in the back of the house." As the tinny voice of Agent Rosario echoed in Amelia's ear, the hairs on the back of her neck rose to attention.

Were they about to spring a trap? Had Sherman led them here on purpose? The tactical agents had swept the perimeter, but they hadn't been able to check for an explosive inside the house.

Amelia was so focused on absorbing her surroundings that the report of Dean's fist pounding even harder on the door almost made her jump out of her skin.

"One more warning. Open the door or we break it down!"

When no movement from within followed, Dean nodded to Tom Harris.

Amelia unholstered her service weapon and moved farther to the side to give Harris and Wilson plenty of maneuvering room. As Amelia pressed a button on her earpiece, Emily Wilson held up three fingers.

"We're about to breach the front door. On the count of three." Amelia waited for Wilson's signal before she started the countdown. By having the agents around the back of the house make their entrance at exactly the same time, they reduced the likelihood that anyone inside would slip through their grasp. "Three, two, one."

Wood splintered beneath the heavy blow of Tom Harris's battering ram, and the sharp *crack* reverberated through the otherwise calm night. On the second swing, the door flew inward, smashing into the drywall behind it with a thud. In one swift movement, Harris shouldered the battering ram and produced his rifle. Emily Wilson was on his heels as he stepped over the threshold, followed quickly by Dean and Amelia.

While Wilson and Harris took a right toward what appeared to be the living room, Amelia and Dean headed down a short hall left of the foyer. Calls of "clear" rang out not far from them as the other agents swept methodically through each room.

With every sense on high alert, Amelia followed Dean into a small bedroom that had been converted into an office. Aside from an abstract painting on the wall and a potted cactus near the window, the space was devoid of decor.

The cactus seemed to provoke Dean. "What's up with the cactuses? Not exactly the state plant."

Amelia considered it. "Endurance."

"What?"

"The cactus is a symbol of strength under harsh circumstances. Enduring Resilience."

"Well, that's...comforting."

Satisfied there was nothing lurking in the shadowy space, they returned to the hall as Dean shouted, "Clear!" Only one of them could fit in the adjacent bathroom, and like the office, it was also unoccupied.

Amelia's adrenaline threatened to fizzle out altogether as the seconds dragged by without incident. Sherman's car was parked outside, but so far, they'd spotted no sign of him anywhere in the house.

Had something tipped him off before their arrival? Had he left his car in the driveway simply to waste their time while he procured another vehicle?

If that was the case, then he had one hell of a head start.

Holding in a sigh, Amelia strode down the hall. "If the blueprints are right, there's a basement around here somewhere. No idea if it's finished or not."

Dean pointed to a shallow alcove coming up on their right. "That should be it."

As they neared the supposed entrance to the basement, Tom Harris emerged from a utility room at the end of the hall. "Nothing in there aside from your usual laundry equipment." He paused, appearing thoughtful. "You know, I might be losing my mind, but I could've sworn I heard something through the vents while I was in there. Sounded like it might've been music. Maybe I'm just getting old."

Neither Amelia nor Dean responded, and for a long moment, the three of them stood in silence as they pooled their collective hearing abilities.

Finally, Dean shook his head. "I don't hear it. Maybe it was just the HVAC?"

Harris pressed his lips together and nodded. "Maybe. All right, let's check and see what's in this basement." He tapped his earpiece. "Walsh, Richmond, I need one of you here at the entrance to the basement. Just need you to check the door."

"Walsh is on his way, Boss."

Footsteps followed almost immediately, and the taller

agent emerged from the direction Amelia and Dean had just come.

"Walsh," Harris murmured, waving the agent forward.

After shining a small flashlight in every crack around the doorframe, tapping the door in a few different places, and pressing his ear to the beige surface, Walsh flashed them a thumbs-up. "It's locked, but I didn't see anything that indicates a trap."

Harris unshouldered the battering ram. "Don't worry, I've got the key."

Agent Walsh grinned and retreated into the hall.

With the first hefty blow, the doorframe shuddered and groaned but didn't give way. Unperturbed, Harris swung the battering ram a second time, with only slightly better results.

Dean's eyebrows knitted together. "What the hell is this thing made of?"

Harris lifted a shoulder. "Probably reinforced from the other side. It just takes a little more effort."

Amelia blew out a long breath, mentally preparing herself for what they were about to face.

True to his word, Harris delivered four more decisive strikes before the lock shattered and the heavy door swung open. Swiping at a sheen of sweat on his forehead, Harris stepped back to make room for Amelia, Dean, and Agent Walsh.

As the ringing in Amelia's ears receded, she caught the first notes of a familiar song.

She glanced at Dean. "Is that...?"

Dean's face was masked with the same level of confusion plaguing Amelia's brain. "Yeah, that's from the opera *Sweeney Todd*."

So Tom Harris wasn't losing his mind or his hearing.

Ignoring the tune, Amelia leveled her service weapon with the set of stairs. Walls on either side of the steps blocked her view of the area below, but she made out the dim glow of a light. With the sights of her Glock leading the way, she started her descent.

The notes of the song grew louder, but panels of sound-proofing foam explained why they hadn't noticed the music from upstairs. Tom had caught a snippet through the vent, but otherwise, the basement was thoroughly insulated from the rest of the house.

After six or so steps, the wall on Amelia's right cut off to reveal a long desk propped up against an expansive pane of glass.

"Holy shit." Dean's interjection was struck with more awe and emotion than Amelia had ever heard.

Amelia was so focused on monitoring the stairs for trip wires and searching the immediate area for a hidden shooter that she'd barely processed the scene on the other side of the wall of glass. With Dean's quiet exclamation, she halted on the second to last step and turned her attention to the transparent wall.

To her horror, Lou Sherman loomed over a prone figure, mostly covered by blue surgical sheets. Aside from the figure's hair color, she couldn't make out much of his appearance.

Not that her attention lingered long on the unconscious man's hair when there was a gaping wound in his lower abdomen.

The gruesome scene didn't end there.

As Lou Sherman's gaze drifted away from the man on the operating table, Amelia spotted the glistening red object in Sherman's bloody hands.

One of the victim's kidneys.

31

A complete loss for words wasn't a common experience for Amelia, but witnessing the primary person of interest in at least six homicides holding the kidney of a man who was still alive—according to the heart rate monitor visible beside his IV stand—was enough to render her speechless for a second or two.

Her mind raced as she fought to bring herself into this bizarre reality like a diver desperate to make it to the surface.

She'd seen suspects who'd pressed a firearm to the temple of a victim in a last-ditch effort to save themselves from being taken to prison. She'd even experienced the aftermath of a psychopath killing one witness after another as he tried to flee a warehouse basement.

But a lunatic holding an innocent person's kidney in his hand while an opera about a butchering barber droned throughout the room? This was most definitely a first.

As Sherman glared daggers, Amelia turned and beckoned for Tom Harris. While the man neared, she lowered her voice to a conspiratorial whisper. "We need a surgeon here ASAP. A real surgeon."

Harris pulled out his cell. "Jammer's offline now. I'll get someone on it right away. What else?"

Amelia glanced over her shoulder to where Sherman was studying her and Harris intently. "The surgeon is our priority. The sooner we get someone here who's capable of stabilizing the vic, the sooner we can haul Sherman out of here."

We just have to keep him from killing the guy in the meantime.

With a curt nod, Harris turned back to Walsh, and Amelia shifted her attention back to Sherman.

Dean pointed to a speaker in the top center of the glass. "There must be a way to activate the speaker from here."

Beside one monitor, Amelia spotted a handful of buttons. She jabbed one beside a little microphone icon, and the speaker at the top of the glass hissed. "Lou Sherman? Step away from the table and keep your hands where I can see them."

"I don't like your tone, Agent." He gestured to Amelia and then to Tom Harris with the hand holding the kidney. "And I don't like how that agent is conspiring with the other one."

You need to do something. Try to figure out what in the hell is going on here, even if all you're doing is buying time.

"Who's the man on the table? What are you doing to him?"

Rather than reply to any of her questions, Sherman merely stared back at her.

"Why isn't he answering?" Dean followed Amelia as she hurried over to the desk.

As Harris and Walsh descended the steps, a series of four-letter words preceded them.

Amelia ignored the men's outbursts as she scanned the desk. A closed laptop rested in the center, along with a couple of monitors, displaying a clear view of the closed-off room. "Maybe he's just being a pain in the ass."

All the while, Lou Sherman stood, kidney in one of his raised hands, his scrutinizing gaze fixed on Amelia and Dean.

Amelia met the psychopath's gaze, her face neutral even as her thoughts moved a million miles per minute. "Lou Sherman. I'm Special Agent Storm with the FBI. I need you to put down that man's kidney."

Put his kidney down? Where? It's not a fucking gun.

Rather than rush to obey the order, Sherman merely glared back at her. "This is an invasion of my privacy, Agent Storm. Doesn't the Fourth Amendment protect me from illegal searches?"

Jaw tightening, Dean slapped the warrant against the glass. "Here's the warrant. Why don't you come on out here so you can take a closer look?"

To Amelia's surprise, Sherman jolted at Dean's sudden movement. "I'll do no such thing. Besides, I don't think you want me to do that." He pointed to a white container beside a handful of bloody surgical tools. "Lloyd's other kidney is in that box right now. Unless I hook him up to dialysis soon, toxins will begin to spill into his blood, causing irreversible damage to his other organ systems."

Amelia already knew what Lou Sherman was capable of, and she hadn't forgotten that an innocent man's life hung in the balance.

Sherman quite literally held Lloyd's life in his hands.

Straightening her back, Amelia didn't let her gaze drift away from Sherman. As terrified as she was for Lloyd's safety, she wouldn't display so much as a hint of weakness. Her assessment of Lou Sherman so far told her he was a shark—the instant he detected blood in the water, he'd rip her to pieces.

Cold professionalism was all he'd get from her. "If you let this man die, you'll have committed a premeditated murder right in front of four FBI agents. We know all about your organ-trafficking business, Mr. Sherman."

"Doctor Sherman!"

Speaking of weaknesses...

Dean offered the doctor a wan smile, his face as expressive as the drywall at their backs. "Your title won't matter much when the U.S. attorney brings you to trial, and you wind up with a needle in your arm."

Sherman huffed. "Not likely. Illinois doesn't employ the death penalty."

"Illinois doesn't, but the federal government sure does." Dean shrugged noncommittally. "Don't take my word for it, though. Set that kidney down and google it."

"Please." Sherman rolled his eyes. "You simpletons don't understand. You don't get it. I'm not a trafficker, all right? I'm a scientist. The work I've done here will change the world. Understanding the limits of human endurance is how we've created devices like ECMO, and my studies will provide data to create even better technology! Can't your small minds fathom it? A world where a person can not only be kept alive entirely by a machine, but where they can *live* with the help of a machine?"

This guy is delusional. He actually thinks he's conducting an experiment.

The real question was how to get through to him.

Could they get through to him? Could they even get *to* him when the door had no handle?

Don't take any chances.

Dean moved his hand underneath the counter, clearly looking for some device to open the door. "What's your plan here, Sherman? Are you going to kill someone right in front of a room full of federal agents? If that's not good enough, we could video call the U.S. attorney so we can expedite that lethal injection for you."

"I'm waiting to hear your answer to my partner's question. What's your plan?" If Amelia kept Sherman talking, he wasn't causing more harm to Lloyd. Though some individuals could survive for as long as a week with next to zero kidney function, she couldn't say the same for a man whose kidneys had just been cut out of his body.

Had Sherman stitched the internal injuries? The incisions in his flesh were plainly visible even on the other side of the glass, but what about the blood vessels and other tissues connecting the kidneys to the rest of Lloyd's body?

The erratic beeps from Lloyd's heart monitor seemed to answer Amelia's questions. Sherman lowered his hands as his head snapped between the monitor and the innocent person he was gutting.

"Found it." Dean pushed a button, and the door slid open.

Amelia rushed out of the control room to the operating theater's door.

"Stop!" Sherman commanded. "You'll contaminate the room. Are you so dense that you would risk this man's life by bringing germs into my sterile operating room?"

Amelia's mind raced through her options. Would Lloyd bleed out from an internal injury while Amelia and Dean fought in vain to reason with a psychopath?

Better yet, what was their alternative? Until a surgeon arrived, Lou Sherman was the only one with enough medical experience to save Lloyd's life. Did Amelia really trust Sherman to sew his victim back up and stabilize him for transport to an actual hospital?

Unlikely. She trusted Lou Sherman as far as she could throw him.

Spotting a pile of neatly folded scrubs, Amelia holstered her gun before donning a suit. Since she didn't immediately spot a sink to wash her hands—not that she had time for five full minutes of scrubbing—she pulled on two pairs of gloves, then a mask. She just had to hope that would be enough to protect Lloyd from contamination.

Thus geared up, she calmly approached Sherman and Lloyd. The operating room door shut behind her at the press of a button from Dean.

"I had some medical training in the military. You want to stabilize him, right?" At Sherman's slight nod, Amelia took another step closer. "Good. Then we can agree on that." Amelia searched the area for potential threats, her eyes landing on the rolling tray of surgical instruments. "I need you to push that tray across the room. Use your foot."

Sherman's hands were still slightly raised, bloody kidney in one of them, as he shoved the cart away from the bedside.

"Great. Now place the kidney in the container with the other organ."

Sherman rested his other hand over the kidney like he was protecting a childhood treasure. He held her gaze, as if weighing his options.

"Medical transport is several minutes away," Dean boomed through the speakers. "We need the patient stabilized, or your death certificate is as good as signed. Do as she says and place the kidney in the container."

Dean's urgent tone pushed Sherman into action. Taking a few small steps, he gently deposited Lloyd's kidney next to the other one.

"Thank you, Doctor Sherman. Now, what do we need to do to stabilize this man?" Amelia again searched the area around the table to assess any threats. Everything seemed innocuous enough. But if he tried anything, the gun in her ankle holster was accessible even if the Glock under the scrubs was not.

Suddenly acting like an actual surgeon and not the psychopath he was, Sherman calmly began clamping vessels and instructing Amelia to do likewise, gesturing and commanding as they worked against the clock. Amelia suspected Sherman was enjoying every minute of ordering around an FBI agent.

As one clamp slipped free of the renal artery, blood spurted rhythmically. Again, the heart rate monitor called out in distress. They were running out of time.

"Shit." Sherman's simple exclamation was all Amelia needed to confirm her suspicions that Lloyd's prognosis was grim.

Keep playing to his ego.

"Doctor Sherman, you are a gifted surgeon. What can we do to save this man?"

Snapping out of his apparent fugue, Sherman leveled his gaze at Amelia. "We need to hook him up to the dialysis machine now. We can't wait for whatever quack you rustled up."

Sherman moved the machine closer and began robotically walking Amelia through the steps. "We don't have time to create the arteriovenous fistula. We have to put a tube into a vein in his neck." Amelia didn't understand most of the terms, but she did recognize that Sherman seemed to be actively working to save Lloyd. Probably because his ego enjoyed strutting its stuff.

Sherman's next statement caused Amelia to tense. "I need to make an incision in his neck. I need the scalpel."

"That's not going to happen." Amelia moved to the surgical tray across the room, picked up the scalpel, and returned to the side of the table. "Tell me what to do."

This would be Amelia Storm's cut. Not his.

Sherman blinked several times, as if he didn't believe what he was hearing. "You're not a trained surgeon. Give me the scalpel."

The sudden thud of the operating room door bursting open surprised Amelia and the psychopath across from her.

Not wanting to take her eyes off Sherman, Amelia had to trust it was one of her team.

Dean's West Virginia accent drifted across the room. "I have my Glock trained on you, Doc. If you so much as twitch in Agent Storm's direction, you'll be dead before you hit the floor."

At that, Sherman's right eyelid began twitching. "You are contaminating the area. If this man dies, it will be from infection, not anything I've done." Meeting Amelia's gaze, Sherman stretched out the palm of his hand. "Scalpel."

Slowly, Amelia handed him the surgical instrument. With lightning dexterity, Sherman set about opening a vein and inserting a tube for the emergency procedure. While he worked, he instructed her to finish packing gauze around the clamp on the renal artery in Lloyd's incision.

The heart rate monitor's return to normal caused Amelia to release the breath she didn't know she was holding.

Sherman's shoulders relaxed as well. He gently placed the scalpel on the bedside before fiddling with a few knobs on the dialysis machine. Once he was satisfied with his work, he took a step back from the table.

Defeat seemed to weigh down Lou Sherman. As he pulled off his bloodied gloves, Agents Walsh and Harris stood to either side of the door at the end of the glass wall. Amelia moved a few steps away and slipped off her own surgical gear before cuffing Sherman's hands behind his back.

Both tactical agents trained their weapons on Sherman as he shuffled through the door by Amelia's side. Rattling off his Miranda rights, Harris prodded him up the stairs.

The steps creaked a moment later, and Amelia expected Tom Harris to emerge. To her surprise, a middle-aged woman clad in dark blue scrubs descended the stairwell with Emily Wilson and another unfamiliar man on her heels.

"Backup just arrived." Wilson offered Amelia and Dean a

grin. "And this is Dr. Leah Bartlett and her nurse. They work in the emergency room in Peoria, and the hospital flew them out here to help stabilize John Doe so we can transport him to a proper operating room."

Amelia could have hugged Emily Wilson, but she tempered her reaction down to an appreciative smile. "John Doe's first name is Lloyd."

He still had a battle ahead of him, but Amelia and the others had reached him in time.

Lou Sherman would not claim another victim. Not tonight, and not ever again.

32

Saul Avery's head was like a block of concrete when he tried to move his neck. His last bit of strength was waning. With far more effort than the motion should have taken, he turned to face Mandy. Her pretty eyes were bloodshot from crying, and she clutched a tissue so tightly her knuckles were white.

As of two days ago, the home health setup had become inadequate to support Saul's failing body. Between his fatigue, weakness, and persistent cough, he'd been miserable. Though Mandy hadn't wanted to return to the hospital at first, she'd realized quickly how much Saul had deteriorated.

He could tell she didn't want to let go.

Throat tight, Saul reached a hand toward her. A new round of tears sprang to her eyes, but she took hold of his hand and scooted closer to the bed.

"I'm sorry, sweetie. I tried. I hung on for as long as I could, but..." Saul paused mid-sentence to catch his breath, wheezing and nearly lapsing into a coughing fit as he inhaled.

"I know. It's okay." She sniffled and dabbed at her nose. "I shouldn't have asked so much from you. You're hurting, and I just…just don't want to see you in pain anymore. I don't want you to go, but I don't want you to hurt."

"You didn't ask too much. I got more time with you, didn't I?" Even as his spirits sank, Saul offered his wife a warm smile.

More than a week had passed since the supplier for Saul's new heart had gone dark. Mandy had searched frantically for any signs of the seller on the dark web, but she'd come up empty. In the event the organ broker had been caught by the police, they didn't want to try too hard to get ahold of him lest they wound up on the receiving end of an undercover FBI operation.

Mandy had tried to find another matching organ, but she hadn't even gotten a bead on a new sale when Saul had suffered a second heart attack.

As soon as he'd awoken in the hospital, Saul had known the end was upon him. In truth, he'd made peace with death shortly after the cardiac event that had led to all these other complications. The only reason he stuck around was for his beloved wife.

But now, as he peered up into her sad eyes, he realized she'd accepted reality.

He squeezed her hand. "There's nothing you can do, honey. You did your best. Please, just spend this time with me now, okay?"

Tears slid down her cheeks. "Yeah. I can do that."

33

As Bogdan stared at the American news article out of Chicago, Illinois, he couldn't decide if he wanted to sink down onto the floor in disappointment, or toss his computer monitor out the window.

"Lou Sherman pleads no contest to six counts of premeditated murder." Bogdan raked a hand through his hair as he read out loud. "As part of a plea deal to avoid the death penalty, Sherman provided the names of ten other victims, along with the approximate locations of their remains."

He'd read the article so many times he could recite it from memory.

Sherman had been Bogdan's ticket to finally establishing himself in the snuff film industry separate from the Russian Bratvas. With the surgeon's unique methods, Bogdan had been so confident he could get a foot firmly in place in the market.

Now here he was. Sherman was behind bars in the United States, and Bogdan was here in Yakutsk where the local Bratva was getting closer to finding him each day. Lately, he'd been hesitant to go outside for fear he'd be recognized and killed.

Where did he go now? To a different part of Russia?

He snorted to himself. "I do not think so. I will have the same problem there that I have here."

Eventually, the Bratva would catch on to his little snuff film business, and they'd seek to stamp out the blip of competition. When they realized he, specifically, was the one behind the videos, odds were good they'd kill him much like they'd murdered his brother.

I have to leave Russia. It's become too risky here.

Drumming his fingers against the desk, Bogdan opened a new web browser and searched for Lou Sherman's case again. He scrolled through a couple of pages of results before he noticed one with a brand-new time stamp. Though he didn't recognize the name of the journalism site, he clicked the link.

An image of Sherman's mug shot appeared beside the first paragraph, and as Bogdan skimmed the text, he realized it was just more of the same. Whoever had reported on the case for this website had lagged a few days behind the rest of the world.

Bogdan propped his chin in one hand as he scrolled to a slideshow of images at the bottom of the page. The first displayed an exterior shot of Sherman's rural property, and the second was another mug shot.

As Bogdan navigated to the third photo, he swore his heart stopped beating for a moment.

The caption to the image read, *An FBI agent escorts Sherman to the Metropolitan Correction Center, Chicago.* Innocuous enough, but Bogdan recognized that FBI agent.

After witnessing the man kill his brother, his face was seared into Bogdan's memory.

A combination of rage and adrenaline roiled in his gut.

Mischa Bukov, the rat who'd killed Bogdan's brother, was a fucking FBI agent. Not only was he an FBI agent, but apparently, he was one of the cops responsible for Lou's arrest.

Bogdan wasn't sure how long he sat and stared at the photo, but somewhere along the line, the decision of where to relocate became as clear as the waters of Lake Baikal.

Lucky for him, he hadn't cancelled his upcoming flight to Chicago.

"I know where you are now, Mischa. I am coming, and I am going to cut off your head and mount it on my wall. But do not worry. I will make you a star first. I want the whole world to watch me slice you into a thousand pieces."

The End
To be continued...

Thank you for reading.
All of the Amelia Storm Series books can be found on Amazon.

ACKNOWLEDGMENTS

How does one properly thank everyone involved in taking a dream and making it a reality? Here goes.

In addition to our families, whose unending support provided the foundation for us to find the time and energy to put these thoughts on paper, we want to thank the editors who polished our words and made them shine.

Many thanks to our publisher for risking taking on two newbies and giving us the confidence to become bona fide authors.

More than anyone, we want to thank you, our readers, for clicking on a couple of nobodies and sharing your most important asset, your time, with this book. We hope with all our hearts we made it worthwhile.

Much love,
Mary & Amy

ABOUT THE AUTHOR

Mary Stone lives among the majestic Blue Ridge Mountains of East Tennessee with her two dogs, four cats, a couple of energetic boys, and a very patient husband.

As a young girl, she would go to bed every night, wondering what type of creature might be lurking underneath. It wasn't until she was older that she learned that the creatures she needed to most fear were human.

Today, she creates vivid stories with courageous, strong heroines and dastardly villains. She invites you to enter her world of serial killers, FBI agents but never damsels in distress. Her female characters can handle themselves, going toe-to-toe with any male character, protagonist or antagonist.

Discover more about Mary Stone on her website.
www.authormarystone.com

Amy Wilson

Having spent her adult life in the heart of Atlanta, her upbringing near the Great Lakes always seems to slip into her writing. After several years as a vet tech, she has dreams of going back to school to be a veterinarian but it seems another dream of hers has come true first. Writing a novel.

Animals and books have always been her favorite things, in addition to her husband, who wanted her to have it all. He's the reason she has time to write. Their two teenage boys fill the rest of her time and help her take care of the mini zoo that now fills their home with laughter...and yes, the occasional poop.

Connect with Mary Online

facebook.com/authormarystone

goodreads.com/AuthorMaryStone

bookbub.com/profile/3378576590

pinterest.com/MaryStoneAuthor